D

The two figures were running toward him, still shooting in clusters. Fargo fired and one figure spun as he went down. The second of the two tried to take aim as Fargo's second shot caught him full in the chest. He went down, and as he did, his finger tightened on the trigger in a last, convulsive reaction. Fargo was flattened down behind a tree.

He stayed, not moving, very aware that there was still one more man out there, the one that had gone off unseen by himself.

It seemed an interminable wait, yet he knew that hardly a minute had passed when the voice broke the silence. "I've got her. I've got the girl," it shouted.

Fargo remained motionless. Was it true? Or was it a clever lie? He stayed completely still, and after another long moment he heard the man snarl, "Say something or I'll break your goddamn arm." Ivy's sharp cry of pain followed. Fargo swore silently. It had been no clever lie. The man shouted again, "Come out or I'll kill her."

Fargo realized that the man had a problem. The man expected Fargo was alive, but he wasn't sure of it. That uncertainty was suddenly his best weapon, Fargo decided.

Fargo stayed silent as he desperately hoped he was playing the right cards. But then he hadn't any other cards to play. . . .

**BE SURE TO READ THE OTHER THRILLING
NOVELS IN THE EXCITING TRAILSMAN SERIES!**

THE TRAILSMAN

185

BULLET HOLE CLAIMS

by

Jon Sharpe

A SIGNET BOOK

SIGNET
Published by the Penguin Group
Penguin Books USA Inc., 375 Hudson Street,
New York, New York 10014, U.S.A.
Penguin Books Ltd, 27 Wrights Lane,
London W8 5TZ, England
Penguin Books Australia Ltd,
Ringwood, Victoria, Australia
Penguin Books Canada Ltd, 10 Alcorn Avenue,
Toronto, Ontario, Canada M4V 3B2
Penguin Books (N.Z.) Ltd, 182–190 Wairau Road,
Auckland 10, New Zealand

Penguin Books Ltd, Registered Offices:
Harmondsworth, Middlesex, England

First published by Signet, an imprint of Dutton Signet,
a division of Penguin Books USA Inc.

First Printing, May, 1997
10 9 8 7 6 5 4 3 2 1

The first chapter of this book originally appeared in *Rocky Mountain Nightmare*,
the one hundred eighty-fourth volume in this series.

 REGISTERED TRADEMARK—MARCA REGISTRADA

Printed in the United States of America

The Trailsman

Beginnings . . . they bend the tree and they mark the man. Skye Fargo was born when he was eighteen. Terror was his midwife, vengeance his first cry. Killing spawned Skye Fargo, ruthless, cold-blooded murder. Out of the acrid smoke of gunpowder still hanging in the air, he rose, cried out a promise never forgotten.

The Trailsman they began to call him all across the West: searcher, scout, hunter, the man who could see where others only looked, his skills for hire but not his soul, the man who lived each day to the fullest, yet trailed each tomorrow. Skye Fargo, the Trailsman, and the seeker who could take the wildness of a land and the wanting of a woman and make them his own.

*1860. The raw, rough, wild land where
the new states of Iowa and Minnesota touched.
This story is based on real events that
prove that where there are no laws,
even good men turn bad. . .*

1

Skye Fargo cursed under his breath as he pulled his muscled body out of the lake. It was such a serene, beautiful spot that he'd let himself forget the single, most important rule in this wild, fierce land. He had let his guard down. He had let the beauty of place and moment dull his usual sense of caution. He had slept at the edge of the lake, and when the warm sun of morning came, he'd slipped into the refreshing water, swam, and washed the trail dust from his body and reveled in the moment. And now, as he stepped almost naked, wearing only BVDs, he saw the six figures waiting for him, figures he would have heard, smelled, or sensed had he been alert.

No Yankton Sioux, no Iowa, Oto, or Osage, he saw but could feel no relief at that as he took in the six men with hoods over their heads, only their eyes visible. Skye Fargo's own eyes flicked to the holster and the Colt lying beside his bedroll, and he silently cursed again, the gun beyond reaching in one, quick dive. He looked at the hooded figures and knew that his near-nakedness was not simply a matter of outer garments. The men dismounted, all except one who stayed on his horse and kept a heavy buffalo rifle trained on him. Fargo moved, edging closer to the

Colt. "That's far enough," a man in a blue-checked shirt said from behind his burlap hood.

"What are you doing in these parts, mister?" another man asked.

"Passing through. It's a free country," Fargo answered.

"Not good enough," the man in the blue-checked shirt answered.

"Going to meet somebody," Fargo said and edged his foot forward.

"We know that," the hooded figure said.

"You do?" Fargo frowned.

"Don't play dumb with us, mister. We know why you're here," the figure said.

Fargo frowned at the hooded figures. "You boys are making some kind of mistake," he said and slid another foot forward.

"You made the mistake, mister, and now we're going to teach you a lesson," the man said. Fargo saw the five figures holster their guns as they started to move toward him. That left only the man in the saddle with a gun out, and he had a bad angle, Fargo saw. Gathering the muscles in his calves and thighs, Fargo rose on the balls of his feet and let the five men come a step closer until they all but obscured the rifleman's sight line. Twisting his body as he went into action, Fargo flung himself forward in a low dive for the Colt where it lay.

He felt the bullet graze his shoulder as he hit the ground, and then the blow came down on the back of his neck. He tried to close his hand around the Colt and felt the leather of the holster when another blow smashed into his head. He rolled, took another smashing blow atop his head, felt the sharp pain, and then the gray curtain coming down over his eyes.

He shook his head, and the curtain half parted. He shook his head again, saw the ground against his face, felt the dampness of it, and then he was being lifted to his feet. The last of the grayness dissipated, and he became aware of the ropes around his wrists. Then his face slammed against the bark of a peachleaf willow. He felt his arms pulled forward, tied around the trunk of the willow, his face and chest pressed tight to the tree as more ropes tied his legs to the tree. He could turn his head enough to see the hooded men in a half circle around the tree.

One man wearing a heavy silver belt buckle held a long horsewhip in his hands. "Go ahead, teach him about coming this way again," another voice said. The man's arm came up, and Fargo felt the whip lash across his naked back. A half cry, half oath fell from his lips as the whip bit into his flesh, a sharp cutting pain that was instantly followed by another lash.

"Give it to him," another voice urged, and the whip lashed across Fargo's back again, the pain a sharp, intense sensation. It was only the beginning, an introduction to a kind of pain he had never before experienced.

"Bastards. What's this all about, damn you?" he called out.

"You know, mister, and you won't be forgetting," the voice answered through its hood.

"You're right about that," Fargo returned and winced as the whip descended across his back, and he felt his flesh quiver with the blow. The man wielding the whip bent to his task with a sadist's pleasure. The lashes whipped into Fargo's back, each bringing a red welt, some opening the skin in long strips. Fargo gritted his teeth with each lash, and the level of pain shot upward with each new blow until pain became the only sensation in the world. Almost the only one. Rage and fury still churned through him as his back became a raw, burning expanse. And still the lashes descended. But the crack of the whip was growing fainter. Not because the blows were weakening, but because waves of dizziness assaulted him and Fargo felt himself growing weak. The whip curled around his shoulders, then moved down to the back of his legs to open new areas of searing pain.

The agony grew worse. He was consumed by pain, and he felt his entire body was afire, and still the whip found new places to land. The men's voices were only dull, unintelligible sounds now, and only the raging anger inside Fargo kept him from losing consciousness. But, finally, he felt his body sag, and then, dimly, he was aware they were cutting him down. He felt himself collapse on the ground, his body being turned onto his raw, burning back, and he managed to cry out in protest. But the whip came again, across his chest and then, in a final explosion of excruciating pain, across his groin. He knew he was trying to draw his legs up as the whipping stopped. He tried to cling to consciousness, but the overwhelming pain defeated even his willpower, and he felt the world slip away, grayness, then blackness descending over him.

He had no idea how long he had lain there, or even if he was still alive. He existed in a void, suspended in a sphere without sense or feeling. He was dead, so far as he knew, without consciousness. But then there was something, a flickering of sensation. It began not with suddenness, not with an explosion of feeling, but with a tiny, creeping awareness. Wetness, first. He felt wetness. Thought wriggled through his dimness. The dead didn't feel wetness. The dead didn't feel anything. The good news pushed through the void, and he would have cheered had he been able to do so. He was alive and wondered if he heard the sound of trumpets. The wetness came again, against his face, soothing and gentle. It was a ridiculously difficult effort for him to force his eyes open, Fargo noted, but he did so. The world began to take form again, shapes coming into focus, a blade of grass, a small stone, a piece of wood. He saw the shapes through one eye as his cheekbone lay against the earth. The cool, gentle wetness came again, across his forehead. He started to lift his head and heard his cry as his entire body seemed to explode in pain. "Oh, Jesus," he half screamed and dropped his face back onto the ground.

He heard a voice then, gentle and full of sympathy. "Easy, easy . . . slowly, very slowly," it said, a sweet, soft voice.

"Oh, God," he groaned as he carefully turned his head as the pain swept over him. He blinked, letting the figure come slowly into focus, as if materializing out of a fog. He saw long blond hair appear, framing a face with a straight, thin nose, light blue eyes, and pale pink lips that formed a wide mouth, a small face that held a wan kind of loveliness. "Who . . . who are you?" he muttered.

"That's not important. Helping you is important," she said, and he saw the wet cloth in her hand. "Do you think you can ride?" she asked.

"I'll ride, no matter what," he said, then started to pick himself up and heard his own half shout. "Oh, Jesus . . . Jesus," he groaned as his entire body erupted in pain, his back afire. But she was beside him, holding him by one arm, helping him to stand. "Oh, God, Jesus . . . damn them, goddamn them," he groaned as he forced himself to stand and felt the agonizing pain. He swayed, glad for her hand supporting him.

"Don't move," she said and swam from his sight as a wave of pain swept over him. He fought away dizziness, and when his vision returned, she was beside him with the Ovaro. "I'll help you up," she said, and he cursed in agony as he pulled himself onto the horse, bent forward in the saddle, and fought off the pain. When he was able to straighten up, he saw her on a short-legged dun-colored mare, holding the Ovaro's reins in one hand. "Hang onto the horn," she said as she slowly moved the horses forward. Excruciating pain shot through Fargo with every step the Ovaro took, but he clung to the saddle horn with both hands and groaned curses. The young woman led the way to the other side of the lake, fading in and out of his sight as he fought off waves of pain. The journey seemed to take days, and he tried to keep his eyes on the long blond hair only a few feet from him.

"Where?" he gasped out.

"A line cabin. Trappers often use it in bad weather," she said and kept the Ovaro at a slow walk alongside her mare. Finally, Fargo looked up and saw a sturdy cabin set back from the water. She was at his side as he slid from the saddle. She held his arm as she led him into the cabin where he saw a single room, neatly tended, and she walked him to the cot against one wall. "I think you'd best lie on your stomach," she said. "That's not as raw as the rest of you."

He lowered himself onto the cot and cursed in pain

as his groin came against the sheet. "Don't move. I'll get a bucket of water," she said. "I've got to clean the blood away." He lay unmoving, listening to her leave and return. He felt her pull away the remaining strands of his shredded BVDs and ever so gently use a wet cloth on his back and legs. Though his skin automatically winced at her every touch, the cool water brought some small measure of relief. Finally, when she stopped, he heard the dismay in her voice. "It's all so terribly raw. I'll go try to find something better than water," she said.

"In my saddlebag, a small bottle, leather covering on it," he said and lay still as she hurried from the cabin to return with the little plug-stoppered bottle. She opened it, poured a little onto her hands, and began to apply the salve gently to the raw skin of his back. He felt the soothing instantly take effect and groaned in gratitude.

"What is it?" the young woman asked.

"Balm of Gilead, wintergreen compress, hyssop, and a touch of lard for thickening," Fargo said. "Best salve for cuts and bruises you'll ever find." He fell silent as her hands moved up and down his back and legs. She had a good touch, softly gentle, and his eyes were only half open when she spoke again.

"Can you turn on your side?" she asked.

"Guess so," he said and used the power in his arms and shoulders to shift onto his side, and she began to apply the ointment to the welts across his groin. He felt her slow, hesitate, and then her fingers touching, lifting where one of the lashes had curled around his organ. Finally, she stopped, and he turned onto his stomach again. "Thank you," he said. "Angels have names, don't they?"

"Abby," she said softly. "Abby Hall." She stepped back, and for the first time he was able to see her fully without waves of pain clouding his vision. He saw a slender, almost wraithlike figure in a blue dress, a figure entirely in keeping with the wan loveliness of her face, narrow-hipped and narrow waisted, small breasts that were completely right on the slender shape. Yet for all her smallish, slight figure fashioned of modest, almost adolescent dimensions, she had a very contained, adult calm that gave her the incongruous quality of a sensuous wood nymph.

"Thank you again, Abby Hall," Fargo said and winced as he moved on the cot.

"You get some sleep," Abby Hall said. "Let the ointment do its work."

"Sleep," he echoed. "Now, that's a real good idea."

"I'll be back tomorrow. You stay right there till I come," the young woman said. "I've put your gun and holster beside the cot, though I'm sure you won't be needing them." He nodded, and it was no effort to let sleep come to him the moment she disappeared from the cabin. He fell into a deep sleep at once. There'd be time to sort out what had happened when the burning, searing pain lessened and allowed other thoughts to take charge.

He slept heavily, despite the pain at his every move, and after morning had come woke to the sound of a horse stopping outside. He reached down with one arm, felt along the floor, and found the holster and the Colt. He had the gun in hand as he lay stomach-down on the couch. The cabin door opened, and with a sigh of relief he saw the slender shape and the long blond hair.

She wore the same blue dress and carried a small

basket in one hand, and he lowered the gun, letting it drop to the floor as he watched her come to the cot. The long blond hair had been freshly brushed and hung loose and full around her small, wan face, and again he had to note the strange incongruity of her, an odd admixture of shyness and sensuousness. "Hello, Skye Fargo," she said, and his eyebrows lifted.

"How do you know my name?" he asked.

"A letter addressed to you in your saddlebag," Abby said, her wide mouth suddenly smiling. "Nothing mysterious," she added, her eyes moving to his back. "How do you feel?" she asked.

"Better, but lousy," he grunted.

Her gaze stayed on his back. "It'll take a lot more healing, but that salve has done wonders. I'll put on some more," she said. He put his head down as she took the bottle and poured out more of the salve, and he felt her hands gently massaging the ointment into the welts and still-raw skin. The ointment soothed, but so did her touch, he realized, long, soft strokes that combined delicacy and firmness. When she had him turn on his side to salve his groin, her touch was less hesitant, he noted, yet just as lingering, and he watched her face as she applied the ointment to his organ, saw her lips part, her eyes taking in the strength of him, her hand staying, on the edge of caressing before she pulled back with suddenness, as though she were afraid of her own thoughts.

He smiled inwardly as he lay back onto his stomach and watched her close the ointment bottle. "It's nice to have your own angel of mercy," he said. "You're very good at this. Practice or natural talent?"

"Not practice," she said quickly. "I've never done anything like this before."

"Never put salve on anybody?"

"Never touched a man like this, all over, I mean, naked and all," she said, and he heard the embarrassment in her voice.

"Somehow, I don't think you mind," he slid at her and saw the pink flush come into her face as she looked away.

"You'll be needing more tomorrow," she said.

"Will you come back to do it?" he asked, and she didn't look at him as she nodded, the pink still suffusing her face.

"I've food for you in the basket," she said.

"You can't stay?" he asked.

"No, not today. I'll stay longer tomorrow," Abby said.

"How did you happen to find me?" Fargo asked.

"I was riding by just before it was over. I stayed behind the trees. There was nothing I could do," she said.

"Just luck, then, for me," Fargo said, and she nodded.

"I had to try to help you after they left," she said. It was an answer that left a lot unanswered, but Fargo decided not to press further and watched her as she let her eyes move over him again before she started to walk from the cabin. She walked with a careless kind of grace, narrow hips swaying rather than swinging, breasts hardly moving at all. He lay still and listened to her ride away as thoughts danced through his mind, pulling together little pieces of what had happened. His attackers could have killed him, but they hadn't. That said something right there. They'd let him stay alive for only one reason, so he could tell others what had happened to him.

But who and why, he asked himself. They had mistaken him for someone he wasn't. Who, and who did they want him to warn? The questions simmered, and he cursed the men who had whipped him within an inch of his life. He wanted to pay them back and answer the questions that crowded his mind. But was it possible to track them down? and was it worth the time and effort? he wondered. He had commitments to meet and places to be. His thoughts went to Abby Hall. Had she really happened by in a stroke of luck? It was possible, yet he had a built-in skepticism about that kind of luck. Or did she know those who had whipped him so mercilessly? Had shame as well as mercy played a part in her helping him? The question didn't make him any less grateful to her, but it persisted in his thoughts as he went to sleep again, the body making its own demands.

He woke when the night was deep, investigated the contents of the basket, and found cold chicken. He listened to the distant call of timber wolves as he ate. He slept afterward until day came and woke with the skin of his back feeling a lot less raw. Abby arrived a few hours later with another basket. She wore a deep green skirt and shirt that, against the blond hair, made her resemble the gracefulness of an evening primrose.

"How is it this morning, Fargo?" she asked.

"Better," he said, and she quickly began to apply the ointment to his back. But he felt a difference in her touch, her fingers moving with longer, slower strokes, almost caressingly where his back had begun to heal. He watched her, and when she came to his groin, her pale pink lips parted again as she made a special effort to concentrate on her task. She had just finished salving the strong, soft-firmness of his organ when he reached up and closed his hand around her wrist. "Stop . . . sit a minute," he said, and she lowered herself to the edge of the cot as he lay onto his stomach. "Tell me about Abby Hall. Where does she go when she leaves me?" he asked.

"Home," Abby said, and he brushed back a lock of the long blond hair and decided there was a definite loveliness to the small face, its wan quality deceptive, masking a quiet strength.

"You've family there?" he questioned.

"Ma and Pa and two brothers. We have a hog farm, mostly polands," she said, leaning back, and he saw the smallish breasts that nonetheless made sweetly definite points in the shirt.

"Tell me, do you know the men who attacked me?" he queried.

"No," she said quickly. Too quickly, he smiled inwardly. "Why would I know that?" she asked.

"You can't live too far away. I wondered if you recognized any of them," Fargo said mildly. She shook her head, but didn't look at him, he noted. "They mistook me for somebody else. You have any idea who it might have been, or why they did?" he continued, and again she shook her head. Fargo decided not to press her further as he saw the tightness touch her wide mouth. The subject bothered her, he saw. Abby knew more than she was telling, and it upset her. He'd wait to see if she'd come to volunteer more, he decided, and put his head down. Finally, she finished and stood up.

"I'll be back in the morning," she said. "Don't forget to eat tonight. It's important to keep your strength up." She gave him a smile, the first she'd given, and there was an almost bashful sweetness in it, and then she paused at the door. "That beautiful horse of yours has been grazing nearby," she said and hurried on. He listened to her leave and settled down on the cot, feeling sleep eager to fling itself over him.

When he woke, the night was deep, but he could feel the healed skin on his back, the burning almost completely gone. He swung from the cot, stood up, and carefully stretched. There were still areas of his back that hurt, and he took slow steps to the cabin door and gazed out. The moon traced a silver path across the lake, and the black-and-white form of the Ovaro quickly appeared and came to the cabin door. He stroked the horse's snout and neck.

"Soon, old friend, soon," he muttered and retreated into the cabin where he was not unhappy to sink down on the cot again. He slept at once, and when morning came, he woke, moved, stretched and felt how much the night's sleep had helped. Abby arrived soon with another basket, paused, and glanced down at the one on the floor.

"You didn't eat," she said reproachfully.

"Slept through. I'll eat later," he said and saw she wore the blue dress again, and he watched the fabric cling to the smallish breasts as she sat on the cot and started to rub on the ointment.

"You are healing quickly. I think in another day you'll be able to put on clothes," she said.

He picked up something in her voice. "You sound disappointed." He smiled and waited, but she didn't answer. "Am I wrong?" he pressed, his voice gentle.

Her voice was almost too soft to hear, and she gave a tiny shrug. "No," she breathed, and he saw her look away. "That's terrible of me, isn't it?" she murmured.

"Which? Feeling that way or admitting it?" he asked.

"Both," she said, a thoughtful furrow touching her smooth brow.

"No, you're just being honest with yourself, and that's always good. Not enough of us are," Fargo said and saw the light blue eyes studying his face.

"I've never done this before," she said.

"Tended to anyone?"

"Touched a man all over, massaged a man," she said.

"Never?"

"A few boys, a little touching, but nothing really. And now, with you, it's all so different," she said. "I'm feeling things I never felt before." She stopped, and a rush of pink flooded her face. "I didn't mean that the way it sounded."

"It's brought out caring, nursing, tenderness, all the wonderful feminine things that are part of you," Fargo said.

"What about the other things I'm feeling?"

"Desire? Wanting? They're as much a part of you as caring and tenderness. They're wonderful, too," he said.

Her eyes stayed on him. "Why here with you? Why are these feelings happening to me now?" she asked.

"Some things make their own time to happen," Fargo said.

"It's like I don't know who I am anymore," Abby said.

"It's called discovering yourself. It can be upsetting," he said as she began to rub ointment onto his back.

"Indeed," she said softly, and he felt the long, slow

22

caressing of her fingers. Finally, when she finished, she rose at once. "I must go," she said, hurrying to the door, head turned away as if she didn't dare look at him again.

He stayed on the cot after she rode away, half slept, and finally rose, went to the door, and watched the day turn to dusk. He stretched, felt the marked improvement in his back, and ate the delicious spiced rabbit in Abby's basket. He found himself thinking more about her than about the men who had whipped him. She had pushed them aside in his thoughts, become her own mystery, a beautifully wan sprite, the strange admixture of shyness and sensualness in her growing stronger with each passing day.

Finally, he returned to the cot, stretched out, and turned thoughts to how he had come to ride the rich, strong land. The note that had brought him still lay in his saddlebag. It had been a long time since he had heard from Ben Brewster, and the letter had brought back a time past he'd never forgotten. He'd never liked Ben Brewster terribly much, but that wasn't important. He was indebted to Ben Brewster, and that was more important than liking the man. And so he had come to answer the letter, a plea he very much wanted to answer, a debt he wanted to pay. He had wondered about being called here. It was not Ben Brewster's kind of land. It was a land too powerful, too raw, too new. In some places it was called Iowa, in others Minnesota. But the land knew nothing of man's arbitrary divisions.

His borders were only marks on a map. The land knew only itself, fertile, rugged, rich in timber and soil and wildlife. The law had long ignored this land, leaving it to pioneers, adventurers, and the red man. It had been left for those to do on their own as best they could. Of course, that would change one day, he knew. Time always brought changes, some for better, some for worse. He stretched again, liked the way his body felt, and went to sleep with a small, wan, and quietly lovely face in his thoughts. When morning came, he rose and felt almost his old self. He rose, went outside, and called the Ovaro to him, took a pair of BVDs from his saddlebag and pulled them on. He was sitting on the edge of the cot when Abby arrived, and her eyes widened when she saw him. "Surprise," he said.

Her little smile held a touch of ruefulness. "Not really," she said.

"I waited for you before going down to the lake. I'd like to swim away all the dried ointment," Fargo said.

She stepped around him, her eyes scanning his back. "Yes, you're almost all healed."

"Come with me," he said, rising and taking her hand, and she gave a half shrug as she walked at his side. "You know, it really hasn't been fair," he said as they halted at the water's edge. "My being naked as a jaybird all these days and you being all proper and covered."

She regarded him thoughtfully as he stepped into the lake. "That was the way of it," she said carefully.

"I know," he said from waist-deep water. "But you could change that."

"Why?" she asked evenly, not returning his smile.

"Because you want to," he said.

The tiny, thoughtful furrow he had come to know touched her brow, and she said nothing for a long moment. Then, without a word, her arms rose, and with one motion she lifted the dress and slip beneath it to fling both garments on the ground. He heard the quick, sharp intake of his own breath as he stared at her. She seemed a wood nymph that had stepped beautifully and unself-consciously naked out of the forest, a vision where less was more and more was unneeded. He saw a new boldness to her as she stood motionless, chin lifted upward, enjoying his enjoyment of her.

2

Enjoyment was the perfect word, Fargo admitted silently as he took in the total loveliness of her slender, half-girl, half-woman body, narrow hips, narrow waist, not an ounce of unneeded flesh on her. The smallish breasts were completely right on her, cups insouciantly upturned, delicately pink little nipples on small, matching areolas, all against shimmeringly white skin. An almost concave abdomen curved down to a fuzzy little triangle, petite and entirely in keeping with the rest of her. She moved forward, stepping into the water, and he watched her breasts sway ever so slightly in perfect unison. She reached him, the boldness still in her eyes, halted, and then slid beneath the surface to emerge with blond hair wet against her shoulders and tiny droplets of water poised on the pink nipples.

Her arms closed around him as he reached down and licked the tiny droplets away as his tongue passed across the pink nipples, and Abby uttered a sharp gasp. Her arms tightened, and she stayed with him as he pushed himself backward into the water, swam, dived, surfaced, turned, and rolled. She stayed against him, and he felt the soft smoothness of her. He rose, found footing, and lifted her in his arms, carrying her from the lake to the cabin. He put her gently on the cot and came down beside her, and her wide mouth was open for him, welcoming, eager, surprising in its intensity. Her tongue darted out, met his, twisted, pulled in and out, and she made tiny, sharp noises, and he knew there was nothing learned or mannered to her, only a selfless openness.

The little sharp noises turned into breathy cries as his lips closed around one upturned breast. He circled the tip, felt the thin, tiny hairs that circled the areola, then let his tongue taste each with a gentle pull, and she cried out happily. He drew the saucy little cup deeper into his mouth, pulled on it, and she gasped out words of pleasure. "Yes, yes, yes . . . more, more," she murmured, and her slender body half twisted, turned, rose, then fell back again, all of her entreating, beckoning. His hand slid downward slowly across the almost concave abdomen, pressed through the small, fuzzy triangle and felt the sizable swell of her Venus mound. Abby's cries grew harsher, more demanding, and when his hand came to the soft portal, he found it warm and flowing. A half scream escaped her, and the wood nymph body slid up and down against him, softly undulating motions, as if she wanted to let every part of her touch him.

"Take me, please . . . oh, take me, take," she whispered as her fuzz-covered Venus mound moved up and down against him. Her slender legs opened, then came around him, and he felt the quiet wildness that had seized her. But no crudeness to her, no blatant flinging herself at him. Her every motion was pure sensuous discovery, the world exploding for her and she reveling in the new pleasures. He brought his own throbbing tumescence to her, let the pulsating tip touch, rest on her quivering cavern. "Aaaiiii . . ." Abby half screamed. "Oh, God, oh God . . . oh wonderful, wonderful." She moved, pushed herself onto him and screamed again as he slid, throbbing, into her, and then her arms were clasped around him, her body pressed tight against him as she moved back and forth with him, gasping, screaming, squealing, crying, every sound another expression of pure pleasure until finally she was with him in a long, quivering rhythm, groaning ecstatically with each slow thrust. She lifted the smallish breasts with her hands, pushing them up to his mouth, where he took in first one, then the other as she made little sounds of extra delight.

Her thin, slight build proved deceptive as she stayed with his every thrust and demanded more, her body, her clutching movements, her high-pitched little gasps all giving evidence of the newfound passion let loose inside her. But, finally, as the body demanded its final ecstasy, he felt her hands beating against him and the sudden franticness in her cries, and then she gave little screams as she tightened around him, every part of her quivering. "Oh, oh, oh . . . oh, oh, oh . . . oh, migod, oh, migod," Abby screamed as she seemed consumed by forces beyond herself, but he knew that ecstasy is always beyond itself, always the unbearable bearable, the ultimate pleasure that sets its own limitations.

When her last cry drifted away, she lay tight against him and kept one saucy breast in his mouth, the flesh unwilling to relinquish pleasure. "Oh, Fargo . . . I never dreamed, never thought, never imagined. . . ." she said, letting the rest trail away.

"It could be this wonderful?" he finished for her as she let the wet, glistening breast slip from his lips, and she nodded vigorously and pressed her face to his chest.

"The day is young yet," she murmured sleepily.

"Relax, first . . . sleep some," he said, and she made a purring noise and was asleep in seconds. He dozed with her, and later, when she woke, he drank in the languid beauty of her, all slender curves, every part of her fitting every other, wood nymph and woman, shy and sensual even in repose. He saw her eyes boring into him, her lips parted, and then he felt her hand sliding down to him, across his groin, taking hold of him, and he felt himself responding at once.

"Oh, yes, yes, yes," Abby breathed, stroked, caressed, and once again the little cabin echoed to her tiny, sharp cries of new discoveries and new ecstasies. Finally, she lay silently beside him and stayed against him as the day drifted toward dusk. When she sat up, the upturned breasts swayed, and he touched their loveliness. "I must go," she murmured.

"Will you be back?" he asked, knowing the answer.

"No. You are healed. It is over. It has been the most wonderful time of my life," she said.

"You can't just ride away. You have things to tell," he said.

"No, I have nothing to tell," she replied.

"You know that's not so," Fargo said gently. "I've questions, some about you. I know you've questions about me."

"They'll not be asked. It is best this way. It was our time. It came to us. I want to remember it that way," she said, pulling on clothes. He watched her and knew he could not press. He might not have made it without her. He owed it to her to do as she wanted.

"I never argue with angels of mercy," he said as he walked to her horse with her.

"Don't come back this way, Fargo," Abby said, her small face grave. "That's the hardest thing I've ever had to say."

"Might be the hardest thing I've ever had to do," he said. "But I can't promise. I've someone to meet. I don't know where that might take me."

"I want to remember you . . . us . . . this way," she said, and her kiss lingered before she tore herself away and climbed onto the dun-colored mare. She rode away, not daring to look back, and he waited till she was out of sight before returning to the cabin. Dusk was on the land, and he decided on another night of rest on the cot. She stayed in his thoughts as he edged toward sleep. Perhaps she was right, he reflected. It was best this way. She'd remain a strange wood nymph from out of nowhere, an incongruous mixture of wan sensuality that would fill its own place in his memories. Not everything needed to be explained, he told himself as he fell off to sleep.

When morning came, he took time to swim in the lake and felt almost completely his old self. Finally, he was on the Ovaro, riding south into Iowa, and, following the instructions in the note in his saddlebag, he made his way to the Raccoon River.

The names of America always held him. They grew out of the land, were a part of the land as surely as the trees, rivers, animals, rocks, and mountains, reflecting the very essence of the growing nation. The Raccoon River was one more testimony to the uniqueness of America's names as he saw the abundance of the clever, curious, spectacle-faced denizens along the low brush of the shoreline. He also saw black bear and grizzly, beaver and white-tailed deer, and heavy flocks of quail. When he reached a tall rock split down the center, he turned west, again following instructions, then crossed a long field of brilliant, scarlet trumpet honeysuckle until the flower dwindled away and the terrain became flat and thick with grama grasses.

The town announced itself by cleared land dotted with cattle corrals and farmhouses that stood guard over plowed fields. Their number surprised him, the area more cultivated than he'd expected. A steplike series of stone formations rose up to give the town its name, Dry Falls. He rode into the main street and saw that the town sported a brick bank and a white-painted town hall, plus the usual saloon and warehouses. The street held a fair amount of traffic, mostly farm wagons with a few Conestogas and buckboards. He was glad that, even with the unexpected delay, he was still a few days early. He found the letter the note had mentioned and dismounted before an old, clapboard, two-story structure that sported a fresh coat of white paint. The interior was a study in dinginess, he noted as he went inside the inn and stopped at the front desk.

A pasty-faced youth looked up at him. "Single, couple of days," Fargo said.

The youth took a single key from the wall behind him. "Second floor," he said.

"Ground floor," Fargo said and caught the flash of craftiness in the youth's eyes.

"That'll cost you extra," the youth said.

Fargo leaned forward, and his hand closed around the youth's shirt. His voice stayed pleasant, but his eyes had become blue quartz. "Do you see the word *rube* on my face, sonny?" he asked.

The youth's face grew even pastier. "No, sir," he said. "No extra charge for ground floor. We don't have that rule anymore. I forgot."

Fargo took the key and released his grip on the youth's shirt. "Glad I helped you remember," he said with a smile. "I'll see to my horse."

"Public stable end of Main Street," the youth said, and Fargo went outside, then walked the horse down the street. He was nearing the end of town when he came upon a woman struggling with a big chestnut stallion. She hung onto the reins as she tried to get onto the horse, but the stallion pulled backward, taking her along. Fargo saw the big stallion's ears laid back, his eyes starting to show whites, but the woman kept pulling hard on him.

"Ease up on him, lady," Fargo shouted.

"I can handle him," the woman snapped, and Fargo saw peroxide blond curls around a not unattractive face despite too much makeup, a full-figured body with a large bust under a dark shirt. "Stop it, you goddamn bastard," she said to the horse and yanked hard again on the reins.

"You won't handle him that way," Fargo said, his eyes on the stallion as the horse's lips lifted and his eyes rolled back in his head. But no fear in him, Fargo saw, only the stubborn anger of a stallion being challenged the wrong way. "He won't give that way," Fargo said. "Calm him down."

"I'll handle him," the woman repeated, shortened her grip on the reins, and yanked hard again. "I know this son of a bitch." She tried to half leap into the saddle, riding britches giving her freedom of movement.

She got one foot in the nearest stirrup when the stallion reared, let out a roar, and whirled. Fargo saw the woman flip onto her back, her foot caught in the stirrup as the horse started to run. With a leaping dive, Fargo landed alongside the stallion's head, curled his one hand around the horse's cheekstrap, and let his weight bring the horse's head down. Digging heels into the ground, he hung on and with his other hand grabbed the reins up tight below the bit and pulled. The stallion backed and tried to shake his head, but Fargo's weight hanging on him stopped that and he came to a halt.

Fargo heard the woman hit the ground as she pulled free of the stirrup, looked back, and saw her picking herself up. "That bastard," she hissed and started toward the horse.

"Back off," Fargo snapped. "Let him calm down. You can't push a stallion head-to-head. You've got to work him around to do what you want."

She stopped, and Fargo saw brown eyes frowning at him, but the fury sliding out of her. The stallion had also calmed down, and Fargo relaxed his hold, stepped back, and let the horse shake its head and blow steam from its nostrils. "I guess I should be thanking you," the woman said, and Fargo nodded and had a moment to properly look at her. He saw full lips, a sensual mouth, and a small nose in a face with heavy cheekbones that just avoided being coarse. Her brown eyes moved across his chiseled features, and he saw instant approval in the way she regarded him. She was in her early thirties, he guessed, a face that knew a lot about passion but little about tenderness, the face of a woman who demanded her own way and knew how to get it. Yet with her ripe figure, she exuded her own brand of allure. "I could've been hurt badly," she conceded.

"More than that if he'd taken off," Fargo said.

"You're new in town," she said, still studying him.

"Paying a visit," he said.

"I'm Lila Davis," she said. He took the hand she held out.

"Skye Fargo," he said. Her hand was still around his when a short, stocky figure ran up, puffing hard, a gold watch fob dangling from the vest under his tweed jacket. Fargo took in the man's coarse, heavy-featured face, heavy lips, and small, sharp eyes, flattened nose, and balding pate.

"Saw it from the warehouse," the man said to the woman. "Dammit, Lila, I told you not to ride that damn horse."

"All's well that ends well," Lila Davis said airily and finally let go of Fargo's hand to gesture to the stocky man. "Burt Davis, my husband," she introduced. "Luckily, Mister Fargo was on hand."

Fargo saw the man's small, sharp eyes narrow at him, throw a glance at the Ovaro, and return to him. "Fargo . . . Skye Fargo. Yes, you're the Trailsman," Burt Davis said.

"Been called that." Fargo nodded.

"I was in Kansas when you finished trailing for Bill Bannion. I remember, and I couldn't forget that Ovaro of yours," Burt Davis said. "What brings you to Dry Falls?"

"Supposed to meet somebody," Fargo said.

"Well, we can give you a much better reason than that," the man said. "And properly thank you for saving Lila's neck. Have dinner with us tonight at our place. This might be a stroke of good luck for all of us."

"Yes, please do," Lila said and somehow managed to make it sound more like a command than an invitation, and he saw her eyes still on him. But the thought of a good dinner had its own appeal.

"Why not?" He shrugged.

"Go south out of town, turn right at the first fork. You can't miss us. Six o'clock?" Davis asked.

"Six it is," Fargo said.

"That'll give you a chance to look around my town," Burt Davis said and laughed as Fargo's brow lifted. Davis turned on his heel and strode away, moving with surprising speed for such a short, stocky figure.

"Modesty isn't one of Burt's attributes," Lila Davis remarked, and Fargo glanced at her.

"You saying it's true?" he questioned.

"Yes," she said. "Burt owns most of what's in town, including the bank and the saloon. The sheriff's his man. So's the judge."

"Guess that makes it his town," Fargo said. "Sounds like you're a lucky woman, being married to a powerful man."

"Burt's real good at some things and real bad at others," she said somewhat cryptically. He gave her a hand up onto the stallion. "Be prompt. Burt turns in early," she said, adding, "but I don't." He watched her ride away, deep breasts bouncing, then walked to the end of town before returning to the inn. He found the room simple but adequate, a single window in one wall and a single bed facing it. He'd taken a shirt from his saddlebag and used the washbasin in the room to freshen up. When he was changed and feeling clean, he slowly rode from town and found the Davis spread, the house a long, low, stone-and-pineboard building.

Two stables and a small bunkhouse were set back from the main house, and he was surprised to see three large corrals filled with longhorns. His second surprise was the presence of at least six rifle-toting guards outside the house. They watched him go to the house, plainly expecting his arrival, and Lila came to the door as he dismounted. Clothed in a dark red dinner dress, a low-cut neckline showed the creamy mounds of her very ample breasts while the rest of the gown clung to her full-hipped figure. "You always dress for dinner?" he asked.

"Whenever I have an excuse." Lila Davis smiled and took his arm as she led him into the house, the softness of her right breast rubbing against him. She led him through a well-furnished living room to a long, wood-paneled dining room. Burt Davis, wearing a red velvet smoking jacket, sat at the head of a table set with gleaming silverware, a bottle of whiskey at his elbow already partially emptied.

"Welcome, Fargo, sit down," Burt Davis exuded, and Lila guided him to a chair and sat down across from him. An elderly man in a white jacket poured drinks at once, and Fargo took a sip of good rye whiskey. "Tell the cook we're ready for dinner," Burt Davis said as he poured himself another drink.

"You dine formally every night?" Fargo inquired.

"Yes. It keeps the cook and the servants busy," the man answered.

"And those guards outside, you keep them busy, too?" Fargo asked.

"Too damn often," Burt Davis said.

"I guess you make a lot of enemies on the way to owning a town," Fargo ventured.

"Unfortunately," Lila interjected. "But that's the way of things. People resent being defeated."

"Or stepped on," Fargo commented dryly, but drew only a wide smile from her as she shifted in her chair, and he saw one deep breast all but fall from the low V of the gown. "Burt told me about you, Fargo," she said. "I didn't know I'd been rescued by someone famous."

"I wouldn't use that word," Fargo demurred.

"Why not? It seems you're the very best at what you do. And you've a reputation for integrity," she said, a mischievous little smile coming to her full lips. "And a few other things that have more to do with pleasure than principle, I'm told."

"Mustn't believe rumors," he said.

"Some rumors are usually true," she said and sat back as the elderly man appeared with a tray and began to serve dinner.

"We want you to take a herd out, break a new trail, Fargo," Burt Davis said as Fargo enjoyed slices of pheasant. The man's words were becoming slurred, Fargo noticed.

"Those longhorns outside?" Fargo asked.

"That's right. Spent a long time bringing them this far," Davis said.

"Where do you want to take them now?" Fargo queried.

"Northwest. Through Minnesota and into the Dakota Territory," Davis said, downing his glass of rye and pouring another.

A frown wrinkled Fargo's brow. "There's nothing

out there for a herd, no shipping depots, no markets with buyers, no trails to any rail lines, no anything."

"I'll look into that later. Right now I want to drive that herd. Exploring, you could say. I've even got my supply wagons ready, chuck wagon, too. I just need a trailsman, and now I've got one," Davis said.

"Not so fast, friend," Fargo said.

"A hundred dollars a day. That's powerful money," Davis said, and Fargo knew surprise flooded his face. He glanced at Lila. She watched with brows slightly lifted in amusement.

"That sure as hell is," Fargo admitted. "But I'm afraid I can't take it. I've got a job waiting."

"What kind of job?" Davis questioned.

"Can't say till I have my meeting," Fargo said.

"They won't be paying what I've offered."

"I'm sure of that," Fargo agreed.

"Then you've no reason not to take my offer," Davis said.

"I said I'd meet. I made a promise," Fargo said.

"Have your meeting and turn them down," Davis insisted.

"I don't go back on my word," Fargo said.

"I'll do more than pay you for breaking trail. I'll give you a chance to be a man of property," Davis said.

"I said my piece," Fargo answered.

"Fargo's a smart man. He'll cooperate. He knows a good offer when he hears it," Lila cut in. Fargo saw her smiling at him with quiet confidence and decided against answering. By the time dinner was finished, talk had turned to other things, and Burt Davis was having trouble talking at all after downing another two drinks. But he managed to pull himself up as tall as his short form permitted.

"I'll be expecting you, Fargo," he said thickly and, staggering, nonetheless made it up the stairway to the second floor. Lila stayed silent until the sound of a door closing drifted down to the dining room.

"He'll be out cold in minutes. He'll stay that way through the night," she said.

"He always like this?" Fargo asked.

"Burt's a very intense person. He's very good at making money and drinking," Lila Davis said.

"He likes drinking. He's not good at it. There's a difference," Fargo said.

"I stand corrected," Lila said.

"You go along with what he is. That's plain," Fargo said.

"I like what it brings me, and I don't care about his drinking. But I do care about what Burt told me about you. I want you to take the job," she said and leaned forward. The low-cut neckline dipped lower, letting him see the deep, creamy breasts almost down to the twin nipples. "I'll give you another reason to take the job," she murmured.

"Just like that?" Fargo smiled.

"It won't be just like that. Believe me," Lila Davis said.

"Where?" Fargo asked evenly.

"In the guest room. I told you, Burt's out for the night," she said. "He won't be coming down."

She waited, her eyes on him. "You that horny?" he asked.

"I told you, Burt's good at making money and drinking. He'd bad at everything else. A woman gets hungry."

"Why me? I'm sure you can find someone around here," Fargo said.

"I wouldn't trust anybody around here. He owns them all. You're a lot of man, the kind I don't usually meet. And I want you to take the job. You can look at me as a bonus," Lila said.

He half shrugged apologetically. "Sorry, the answer's still no."

Her eyes narrowed at him. "You don't seem a man who'd turn down this kind of offer," she said.

"I don't usually," Fargo said, almost seeing a thin coating of ice form on her face.

"Why now?" she said tightly.

"I get careful once in a while. Instinct, a special sense about women I've developed," Fargo said.

"What do you mean 'a special sense'?"

"Riverboat captains develop a river sense that tells them about the river when seeing, hearing, and smelling isn't enough. A trailsman develops a trail sense, an inner feeling for the things he can't spell out. It goes for women. Some are all pleasure. Some are all trouble. I call it pussy sense."

"And I'm all trouble?" Lila murmured.

"In spades."

"Bastard," she hissed.

"Sorry, honey. Trail sense, river sense, pussy sense. I follow it."

"You won't know what trouble is if you don't cooperate, Fargo," Lila said.

"With Burt or you?"

"Both of us," she snapped. "I always get what I want."

"I still don't go back on my word. Thanks for dinner." Fargo said and rose to his feet. "It was sure interesting." He turned and started from the table when her scream split the air, piercingly loud, a scream that carried outside the house. He whirled at her. She screamed again and let words follow, each screamed out with shattering power.

"Help me, help me. He's attacking me. No, stop . . . no, please stop. Help me."

The cries were delivered with anguished intensity, filled with terror, and he stared at her as she sat unmoving in the chair. "Goddamn bitch," Fargo bit out, then started for her to close his hand over her mouth, but he heard footsteps running to the house and then the front door flung open. Lila got to her feet and pulled the dress from one shoulder to expose one, deep, creamy breast with a large, deep red nipple. She screamed again. "Goddammit," Fargo growled as he ran past her for the half-open windows at the other side of the room. He didn't stop to push the window open further as he lowered himself and dove headfirst out the bottom. He heard a bullet slam into the wall of the room as he hit the ground, and then Lila's voice.

"Don't shoot him. I want him alive," she shouted, and Fargo bounded to his feet and streaked around the house. He reached the front where the Ovaro was tethered, and saw one of the guards, rifle in hand, standing at the doorway. He was peering into the house, and when he heard Fargo and started to turn, it was too late. Fargo's blow smashed into the side of his face, and he went down. Jumping over him, Fargo ran, vaulted onto the Ovaro, and was galloping from the house when the others came around.

He disappeared into the night before they had a chance to reach their horses. He headed for Dry Falls and the inn. They'd expect him to run. Besides, they didn't know he had a room at the inn. It was the best place to hole up for a few hours, he decided. When he reached the inn, he tethered the Ovaro at the back of the house, went to the room, and lay down on the cot in the darkness. Burt and Lila Davis lingered in the night. He wanted a trailsman. She wanted that and more. They were more than a strange pair. He pursued his goals with a dogged determination; she added something close to desperation. Others had known of his reputation and wanted his talents, but not like this, Fargo reflected.

He wanted to find an explanation as the night moved on, but came up with nothing that satisfied, and as the first light of dawn touched the window, he rose from the cot. They had likely stopped chasing after him. It was time to leave. Ben Brewster would be coming to meet him, and he wouldn't be waiting there. He'd have to find a way to track down Ben, Fargo muttered. He'd work on that after he put some distance between himself and Lila and Burt Davis. He opened the door carefully, his body stiffening as he looked out at the four men waiting in the hallway just outside. He flung himself backward as he kicked the door shut and yanked the Colt from its holster. "Sonofabitch," he swore aloud. He'd guessed wrong. They'd chased after him and then come here. But no hail of bullets burst through the door as he crouched on the floor. Instead, the voice called to him.

"This is Sheriff Dilbert. Come out, mister. Keep your gun holstered and your hands in the air," the sheriff said. Fargo moved across the room in three long strides, opened the window, and saw four more men waiting just outside, three holding rifles. He stepped back and cursed again. The sheriff called from beyond the door. "Just come out, mister. Nobody's out to shoot you. You'll get a chance to speak your piece," the man said.

"I'll get a chance to be hanged, too," Fargo answered.

"Depends on what Judge Hennessy thinks," the sheriff said. "But you get a bellyful of bullets if you don't come out, that's for sure."

Fargo swore silently. Hot lead or a cold rope. It wasn't much of a choice. But he'd buy a little time. It was his only option. He holstered the Colt and slowly pulled the door open, then stepped outside where his gun was yanked from its holster at once. Sheriff Dilbert turned out to be a dour-faced man with graying hair and a thin, gangly body. "Lock him up," the sheriff said to his men, who immediately began to pull Fargo along.

"Thought I was going to get a chance to speak my piece," Fargo said.

"Soon as you're behind bars," Sheriff Dilbert said, and Fargo fell silent as he was led down the street. Someone led the Ovaro along, he noted, and soon Fargo found himself inside a small jail cell as the door clanged shut. "Talk, mister," Sheriff Dilbert said.

"Didn't touch her," Fargo said.

"Lila Davis is a fine woman. You calling her a liar?" The sheriff frowned.

"I sure am," Fargo said.

"We'll have to add defamation of character to assault," Sheriff Dilbert said pompously.

"Why not. You're owned, I hear," Fargo said.

"Insulting a town officer. We'll add that," the sheriff thundered.

"Add whatever you like," Fargo grunted, and the sheriff turned away.

"We'll be taking you to Judge Hennessy's court in an hour," the sheriff said and strode from the jail, his men following. Alone in the building, Fargo examined the small, barred window, tested it for loose bars, and found none. The thin, double-edged throwing knife rested inside its calf holster around his leg. He'd leave it there until the right moment came. Freedom would depend on that, so he sat down on the edge of the hard cot and waited. It wasn't a long wait. They returned for him in little more than an hour. Sheriff Dilbert and three of his deputies marched him from the jail, down Main Street, already crowded with horse and foot traffic, to a square building. Led inside, Fargo saw a row of benches facing a heavy wooden table behind which a man sat wearing a black frock coat and black ribbon tie, a book and a gavel at his side. "Judge Hennessy," the sheriff called out, and Fargo took in a man with the red-veined, puffy face of a chronic alcoholic.

Fargo watched a half-dozen figures come into the makeshift courtroom, plainly drawn by curiosity. An old woman carrying a basket sat down in the front row as did three men in work outfits. Another old man using a cane settled himself on one of the benches. Three more of the sheriff's deputies entered, each wearing a badge. It was only then that Fargo noticed the young woman sitting down on the last bench, an even-featured, not unattractive face, brown hair pulled atop her head in a bun. She wore a dark brown jacket and skirt with brown riding boots.

Judge Hennessy banged the gavel, and Fargo turned his attention to the man. "Court is in session," the judge announced. He wheezed between breaths, Fargo noted. "You Skye Fargo?" he asked.

"Last time I looked," Fargo said.

"You've some serious charges here against you," the judge said. "Defamation of character. Insulting a town officer. Assaulting a woman. Defamation of character can get you two years. Insulting a town officer three years. Assaulting proper womenfolk in this town's a hanging offense."

"What about improper ones?" Fargo asked blandly.

"They're on their own. Lila Davis is a right proper woman," Hennessy said.

"If you say so."

"I do. Sheriff Dilbert says you deny assaulting her."

"I do," Fargo said.

"Can you prove you didn't do it?" Hennessy questioned.

"Just my word," Fargo said.

"Against the word of a fine, upstanding woman such as Lila Davis? That's not good enough," Hennessy snapped.

"I had a feeling you'd say that," Fargo grunted.

"Why'd you run?" the judge asked.

"To avoid getting shot. Nobody was about to listen," Fargo said.

"Not good enough," the judge said.

"Where's fine, upstanding Lila? Isn't she supposed to be here?"

"She's filed the charges," the judge said.

"I've got a right to face her," Fargo said.

"Only if there's a trial, and I don't see this case needs a trial. It's open and shut," the judge said.

"And this court's a goddamn joke," Fargo said.

The judge's red face grew a shade redder. "I find

you guilty as charged. Sentence is hanging," he said and banged his gavel on the table.

"When?" Fargo threw back.

"You in a hurry for a rope?" the judge said and frowned.

"A man's got a right to know," Fargo said.

"You'll know. Haven't made up my mind yet," Hennessy said.

"You mean you've got to wait for orders," Fargo said.

"Get him out of here, dammit," the judge thundered as he wheezed, and Fargo felt the deputies start to pull him from the courtroom. He threw a glance back at the rear bench. The young woman was still there, watching intently, a furrow creasing her brow.

3

He was led back to the jail cell where two of the deputies stayed in the small, outer office while the sheriff disappeared. Fargo's eyes narrowed as he peered out at the two deputies. It was all going to come down to the single right moment, and the knife in his calf holster seemed to throb. But the moment wasn't here yet, Fargo saw as the deputies stayed away from the cell. He'd wait till there was only one, Fargo decided, and he sat down on the edge of the cot and found himself thinking about the young woman in the brown jacket. She didn't seem the type to sit in any courtroom out of idle curiosity, and certainly not the farcical one Judge Hennessy presided over. He was still wondering about her when Sheriff Dilbert returned to the jail. He strode almost to the bars of Fargo's cell.

"On your feet," the sheriff barked. "You're getting a visitor." Fargo's brows rose in question. "Lila Davis, though I can't understand why she'd come visiting the likes of you," the sheriff said.

"You said she's a fine upstanding woman," Fargo remarked and drew a glare from Sheriff Dilbert as he turned away to join his deputies.

"We'll all be just outside the door," the sheriff warned and left with his two men in tow.

"And I'm behind these bars. What could happen?" Fargo called after him as his thoughts went to the calf holster. Lifting the leg of his Levi's, Fargo pulled out the thin-bladed dagger and pushed it inside his shirt. That exact moment might be about to offer itself, he muttered as the front door opened. Lila entered the jail, looking proper in a white blouse with ruffles down the front from a high neck. But the deep breasts that drew the blouse tight destroyed the modesty of the ruffles. She halted, almost touching the cell bars, a smug smile forming on her full, sensual lips. "You seem pleased with yourself," Fargo said.

"I told you I always get what I want," Lila Davis said, the half smile staying on her lips. "And now things have become real simple for you."

"How's that?" Fargo asked.

"You do what I want, or I let the judge carry out his sentence," Lila Davis said. "Simple."

Fargo frowned at her, his eyes peering into the wide face and the smug smile. "You'd go through with it, wouldn't you?" he murmured.

"Count on it," Lila said.

He met her waiting eyes with the little dots of smug amusement in their depths. "I take care of you, when you say and how you say, and I break trail for Burt," Fargo spelled out.

"Exactly," Lila Davis said.

"You're part of what he does, but he's no part of what you do," Fargo continued.

"Right again," she said.

Fargo felt the knife against the skin of his chest. His thoughts raced. He'd shoot one arm through the cell bars, close his hand around the ruffled blouse, and yank Lila to him. The knife would be at her throat instantly. But he swore to himself. He'd still have to fight his way out holding her as a hostage, a venture with no guarantee of success. He'd buy more time, he decided. "Guess a man would be a damn fool to turn down your offer," he said.

"He would, and I'm sure you're no damn fool," she said, the little confident smile staying on her lips.

"How do you figure to do this?" Fargo asked, more than idly curious. "You have me practically hanged. How are you going to unhang me?"

"You leave that to me. Do we have a deal, Fargo?" she questioned.

He uttered a grim snort. "We do. You're one determined lady," he said. "Tell me, who comes first, you or Burt?"

"I come first. It'll sort of seal our deal, kind of a handshake, only better," she said, anticipation dancing in her eyes. "I'll be in touch." He watched her walk from the jail, confident and plainly pleased with herself. He'd let her revel in her smugness, confident she'd taught him a lesson. But he'd teach the final lesson, he promised himself as he sat down on the cot.

It was past midafternoon when the jail door opened again and Sheriff Dilbert came in, keys dangling from one hand. "You're one lucky varmint," he said as he unlocked the cell door. "You're free to go, thanks to Lila Davis. I told you she was a fine, upstanding woman."

"I agreed with you. And Burt Davis is a fine, upstanding man," Fargo said. "What exactly happened?"

"She explained how she couldn't be sure you were the man that tried to assault her," the sheriff said. "She said she went into the kitchen and was grabbed from behind. She never did get a look at him, could've been somebody who sneaked in. It seems he threw her to the ground. When she screamed and the shooting started, she saw you run. She figured you were the one, but as she thought about it she realized she could've been wrong. Not many women would have been so fair about it."

"Not many." Fargo nodded soberly as the sheriff handed the Colt back to him.

"Your horse is outside," the sheriff muttered.

Fargo nodded and paused at the door. "There was a young woman in the courtroom, brown outfit. You know her?" he asked.

"Never saw her before. Thought maybe she was a friend of yours," the sheriff answered.

"Nope," Fargo said and went outside where he pulled himself onto the Ovaro. The day was beginning to slide toward dusk as he reached the end of town. He passed the last building, a large, abandoned warehouse, when Lila rode from behind the structure. He halted as she came alongside him. "You're good with words," he said with grudging admiration. "You pulled it all together real smoothly."

"I'm good with everything," she said.

"You sell Burt the same story?" Fargo asked.

"Yes," she said, quiet satisfaction in her face.

"He always buy everything you say?" Fargo pressed.

"Always," Lila said. "But I didn't come to talk about Burt. Be at my place. Ten o'clock. I'll arrange for you to get in."

"Not your place," Fargo said.

"It'll be all right. I told you, I'll take care of everything," Lila said.

"No. I'll keep remembering the last time at your place," Fargo said stubbornly.

"I like to be comfortable," she said.

"My sleeping bag's comfortable," Fargo said. "You'll have to get used to it if we'll be in it on the trail."

She thought for a moment. "Perhaps so," she conceded.

"Meet me behind the house. There's a big stand of blue beech, if I remember right," he said.

"You do. All right, ten o'clock," she agreed, and he watched her ride away as night descended, his jaw muscles twitching. She would have let him hang if he hadn't given in to her. He had no doubt of that. Maybe she was horny, but not that horny. There was more, another reason. She wanted him to screw her, but she wanted to have him breaking trail as much as Burt Davis did. Loyalty? He uttered a wry snort. It was not a word he could associate with Lila. Consuming self-interest was a lot closer to the mark. But she was a special case and deserved special treatment, and he allowed himself a grim smile as he turned the horse back to town.

He drew up before the saloon and went inside, suddenly aware he was hungry. His glance swept a large room with a bar at one side already crowded with customers. A large woman with bottle-blond hair and a buxom figure barely encased in a black gown was plainly in charge of some six skimpily clad girls and the bartender behind the bar. She greeted him with a practiced eye and a mechanical smile. "Hello, handsome. What's your pleasure?" she tossed at him.

"Something to eat and a bourbon," Fargo said.

"We can take care of that," the woman said and

tossed a glance at one of the girls. "Something more, too, if you've a mind."

"Not tonight," Fargo said, and the woman barked orders at the girl who hurried away. The woman moved across the room, keeping an eye on customers and girls, and Fargo sat down at one of the smaller tables. His bourbon came first, then a sandwich of buffalo and onion. He was halfway through with his meal when a figure entered and approached the woman with a shuffling hesitancy. Fargo saw the man's tattered clothing, his unkempt, graying hair, and eyes that had long parted with any self-respect.

"What are you doing here, Charley?" the woman asked gruffly. "You know you're not supposed to be in here."

"Want a meal. I've money for it," the man said and held the coins out in his palm.

"Dammit, you know I'm not supposed to serve you, Charley," the woman said.

"I'd have to walk two miles to the half-breed's place for one of those lousy stews of his. I worked all day in old man Hester's fields for the money. I'm too tired to walk two miles for slop," the tattered figure said. "I've got the money and I want to be served."

"Burt's orders, Charley. You know that," the woman said.

"Fuck Burt Davis," the man said and slammed the money onto the table. "Come on, Gertie, give me something to eat, for old times' sake."

Fargo watched the woman tighten her lips, then nod to one of the girls. "Get him whatever he wants," she said.

"Like hell, Gertie," a voice interrupted, and Fargo saw a big, beefy-faced man step from beside the bar.

"You know Burt's orders. You don't ever serve him a goddamn thing."

The tattered figure turned to the big man. "You've no right to turn away a paying customer," he said.

"Shut up and get out of here," the man said, advancing, and Fargo saw the tattered figure draw himself straighter, his voice quavering as he answered.

"No. You've no right, no right at all. I'm hungry and I want a meal," he said. "Tell him, Gertie."

The beefy-faced man started for the smaller figure, and Fargo saw he had wide, powerful shoulders despite his extra weight. "I'll show you what right you've got, Charley," the man growled.

"He's right, mister," Fargo said, and the beefy-faced man halted and frowned.

"What's that?"

"I said he's right. You've no cause to turn him away. Serve the man his meal," Fargo said between bites of his sandwich. Out of the corner of his eye he saw the beefy figure change direction and come toward him.

"You ever hear of minding your own goddamn business?" the man growled, stopping to loom over the table as the saloon fell silent. Fargo finished the last bite of his sandwich.

"You ever hear of doing what's right?" he said, not looking up.

"I'll show you what's right around here, bigmouth," the man exploded, shooting out one big hand to close it around Fargo's throat. But Fargo pulled his head sideways, and the man's hand closed around air. At the same instant, Fargo shot out a short, straight left that sank into the man's paunch. A rush of air came from the man's mouth as he went backward.

"Goddamn. Sonofabitch," he roared as his breath returned, and Fargo saw him charge forward, arms raised, lips twisted in fury. Fargo rose, got his arms up, and blocked two roundhouse blows, ducked a third, and danced away.

"Simmer down. There's no need for this," Fargo said placatingly. But the beefy figure was in no mood to calm down.

"I'm gonna break you in little pieces, mister," he said and launched a sweeping right that Fargo easily ducked as he moved back. The man came on, sending a whipping uppercut with more speed than Fargo expected, and he felt it graze his jaw as he pulled away. He dropped into a low crouch and shot out a left hook that caught the man charging in again. He followed with a short but powerful right that rocked the man back on his heels. With a roar of fury and frustration, the man charged again, arms shooting out in a wild barrage of blows. Fargo blocked some, ducked away from others, dropped low, and shot a whistling left that stopped the man in his tracks. His right cross caught the man on the point of the jaw and he went down, hitting the ground with a thud.

"Enough?" Fargo said as the man pulled himself to one knee, his face a mask of fury.

"You're a dead man, you bastard," the man spit out, pushing to his feet, and Fargo saw his hand reach down for his gun.

"No . . . don't do it," Fargo said, but the man's face twisted into a savage grin.

"Too late, sonofabitch," he snarled.

He had his gun clear of its holster when Fargo drew, his hand moving with the speed of a rattler's strike. The Colt barked first. Astonishment held the man's face for a fleeting moment before it gave way to the realization of death. His mouth fell open, and he sank to the floor as his last breath left him.

"Damn fool," Fargo muttered.

"Jesus," Fargo heard the woman breathe as he holstered the Colt. "You killed Ernie Gimbel."

"Who's that?" Fargo frowned.

"Burt Davis's top gun," Gertie breathed.

"Wasn't my call. I told him to back off," Fargo said.

"You did," the woman admitted and motioned to the onlookers. "Get him out of here. Take him to the undertaker's parlor."

Four of the men came forward and half pulled, half carried the man away.

Charley's voice cut in. "I still want that meal," he said with a combination of truculence and triumph.

"Get him his damn sandwich," the woman said to one of the girls, then turned to Fargo. "You've stirred up a hornet's nest, mister," she said.

"He pushed it," Fargo said.

"Still, I wouldn't be around when Burt comes to town in the morning," she said.

"I'll remember that," Fargo said, and the girl reappeared with the sandwich. Charley took a bite at once.

"Don't make trouble for me, Charley. Go somewhere else and eat. Some bastard will report everything to Burt," the woman said.

"Sure, Gertie," Charley said, started for the door, and paused to glance at Fargo. "Thanks, mister. Thanks a lot."

"I'll come along," Fargo said and walked beside the man as he left the saloon. Outside, he led the Ovaro behind him as he accompanied Charley to an old shed just past the end of town. "You want to tell me what that was all about?" Fargo asked.

"We'll talk inside," Charley said, and Fargo followed into the shed where Charley turned on a lamp. Fargo saw, with surprise, a relatively neat interior with one wall of the shed filled with books and newspapers. A cot and two battered chairs comprised the shed's furniture, and Fargo lowered himself onto one of the chairs as Charley finished his sandwich. "You're wondering what Burt Davis has against me," the man said.

"That's a good start." Fargo nodded.

"Would you believe I once owned the saloon? Gertie worked for me," Charley said.

"What happened?" Fargo asked.

"Burt Davis talked me into taking him on as a partner. Then he cheated me out of the saloon and everything else I had. That's how he operates. He's lied, cheated, tricked, muscled, and murdered his way to owning the whole goddamn town," Charley said.

"Why aren't you allowed in the saloon?"

"I was too well known. He couldn't just murder me or have me disappear like some of the others. So he's tried to force me to leave town. He's made it impossible for folks to do anything for me. Only I'm stubborn. I keep hanging in, but I don't know's I can go on much longer. He'll probably get his way one of these days."

"How does Lila Davis fit in with all this?" Fargo queried.

"She does whatever will help Burt. She's a woman who knows which side her bread is buttered on," Charley said.

Fargo grunted in agreement as he rose. "Good luck, whatever you decide," he offered.

"Thanks again for standing up for me. Nobody in town dares do it," the man said and closed the door of the shed as Fargo rode away.

Cutting through the center of town, Fargo rode slowly toward the Davis place as thoughts turned in his mind. What had happened hadn't changed anything, not his plans nor the problem of how to contact Ben Brewster and stay away from the Davises. He was still wrestling with the problem when he reached the Davis place, skirted the house, and glimpsed the guards still in place. He reached the stand of blue beech behind the house from the side to see Lila there, wrapped in a dark green, thick robe that reached to the ground.

"You're late," she said, working to keep an edge from her voice.

"You're early," he said.

She shrugged and let a provocative smile touch her sensual lips. "Anticipation," she murmured and fell into step beside him as he walked deeper into the trees. There was nothing under the robe except her, he wagered as he watched the sway of the deep breasts as she walked. He found a spot with a thick canopy of the small, shiny, dark green leaves that marked the blue beech and a half circle of soft club moss to cushion the ground. He sank down, pulling her with him. "What happened to your sleeping bag?" Lila Davis asked.

"Later. Right now I figure that thick robe of yours will do. We don't want to waste time, do we?" Fargo said.

"No, we don't," Lila said as Fargo pulled off his

shirt, and he saw Lila's eyes move over his muscled torso with anticipation and approval. He pulled on the belt of her robe, and it fell open. His guess had been right, he saw as she lay back in full, naked earthiness, her figure slightly overblown everywhere yet throbbing with voluptuousness. He lingered on the large, deep breasts that just avoided being flabby, each tipped with a dark red circle and a large, dark red nipple already firmly pushing upward. Below the deep breasts, a round rib cage curved into a slightly thick waist, a convex belly that slid down to a very bushy, very black triangle.

Full thighs, a few pounds too heavy, still managed to retain a fleshy shapeliness. Altogether, Lila exuded an unsubtle sensuousness that came as much from within as without. He turned, brought his face down to the deep breasts, let his mouth find one large nipple. "Oh, Jesus . . . yes, oh, yes, oh God, yes," Lila cried out at once, and he heard the fervent eagerness in her voice. He pulled on the big nipple, sucked it deeper into his mouth, and Lila's hands hit against his back, and he felt her wide hips lift. "Yes, yes, go on . . . harder, harder," she murmured and quivered as he responded. His hand moved down to press the soft mound of her belly, down further to push through the very bushy triangle to feel the soft malleableness of her pubic mound covered with an extra layer of fat. "God, yes, go on, go on . . . oh, go on," Lila Davis gasped out. He felt the desperation of her hunger as she lifted her hips, let them fall back, then lifted again.

He rubbed the very soft pubic mound, and Lila's full thighs flew apart as she surged her torso forward and upward. She was making deep, groaning, entreating sounds, and the desperate hunger of her brought its own brand of excitement, an erotic desperation that swept everything along with it, and he felt himself responding. He half rose to his knees, lowered his Levi's, and saw her eyes fasten on his beautifully erect offering. "Oh, Jesus . . . ah . . . ah, yes, give me, give me," Lila Davis gasped, reached out for him, closed her fingers around him, and gave a deep groan of delight. She pulled him with her as she fell back, guiding him, holding her thighs apart. "Give me, oh, Jesus, give me," she almost screamed, and he saw her big breasts fall from side to side as her torso twisted. Her eyes stared with a terrible intensity. Her lips parted, working soundlessly, and deep groans seemed to come of themselves from inside her. "Yes, yes, yes . . . now, now, oh, God, yes," she gasped.

He moved and rested his throbbing organ against the large opening as she pushed her pelvis upward. He let himself touch deeper, and Lila cried out in eager delight. She pushed upward again, surging spasms of desire, and Fargo felt his lips pull back, surprised at how much effort it was going to take him. Lila's panting, consuming, earthy sensuousness reached out with its own power, enveloping, demanding to be satisfied, exuding a field of excitement. But with a silent curse, he pulled back, pushed to his feet, and drew his Levi's up as he grabbed hold of his shirt. He saw Lila's eyes staring at him. "What . . . what are you doing?" she gasped.

"Changed my mind. See you sometime, honey," Fargo said as he stepped back. He saw Lila's eyes continue to stare at him, her mouth falling open, and a frown starting to pull at her brow.

"No. No, you can't," Lila said, her voice gathering

strength as realization began to sink in, her frown deepening. "You can't. No, you wouldn't. No, you sonofabitch," she said. Fargo tossed a smile back at her as he vanished into the trees, saw the disbelief in her face turning to a kind of stupendous fury. "God-damn you. Goddamn you," she screamed. "You bastard. I'll kill you." She was still screaming, curses and high-pitched wails of wordless fury intermingling, as he reached the Ovaro and vaulted into the saddle. Her screams grew more piercing as she pushed to her feet. They carried through the trees to the house, he knew. The guards would be running to meet her, and he spurred the Ovaro into a sharp left and raced from the trees. As he emerged near the road, he saw a horse and rider burst from the trees. The Colt instantly flew into his hands before he discerned the brown hair pulled up in a bun.

"This way," the young woman said and spun her horse to the right. Fargo followed and caught up to her as she led into a cluster of hackberry on the other side of the road. "There's a ravine hidden away. I came onto it by accident," she said, turned again, and went down a pathway that ended in a short, narrow ravine heavily covered by the hackberry. "We can stay here till they've done chasing about," she said.

"Thanks," Fargo said and peered at her in the dim light of the ravine. She had a somewhat severe line to her face, he noted, but she was otherwise quietly attractive. "Now, you mind telling me who the hell you are and how you came to be waiting outside?" Fargo asked.

Her eyes were cool and contained as she returned his gaze. "Which do you want answered first?" she asked.

"Let's start with you," Fargo said.

"Ivy Evanston. Ben Brewster sent me to meet you," the young woman said.

Fargo's brows rose. "Is that why you popped up in court?"

"I was on my way to find you at the inn when I saw them hauling you away. I followed," Ivy Evanston said.

"How'd you know it was me?" Fargo queried.

"Ben described you and your Ovaro," Ivy said.

"So much for that. Now, why were you out here, Ivy?" Fargo questioned.

"I left after the judge sentenced you. I really didn't know what to do. I decided I'd go back and try to make contact with you. I thought they might allow me to visit you. I was on my way when I saw you meet your friend and go into the trees with her. I was surprised, to say the least. Are you always being led off by someone?" He ignored the edge of sarcasm in the question.

"No, and she's not my friend," Fargo said.

"Apparently not now, at least," Ivy Evanston remarked coolly. "I assumed you and she weren't going into the trees to play cards, and decided to wait till you came out. I didn't expect to hear her screaming at you." Her sarcasm had taken on a note of acid humor. "Did you perform that poorly?" she slid at him.

"I didn't perform at all. That's why she was so goddamn mad. She didn't get what she was waiting to get," Fargo snapped.

Ivy Evanston's cool stare remained. "Oh? Reticence or impotence?" she asked.

"You're a smart-ass," Fargo growled. "Neither. It was on purpose."

Her brows lifted. "Revenge by denial. That's a twist," she said. "She must have really hit hard at you."

"Let's say I don't like a noose dangled over me. I figured she deserved something special," Fargo said. Ivy Evanston allowed a wry smile to touch her lips. "How come Ben sent you to meet me?" Fargo questioned.

"I'm his assistant," Ivy said.

"Assistant for what?"

"He's the government land agent in this territory. Didn't you know that?"

"Land agent?" Fargo echoed with a burst of harsh laughter.

"That's right. Why do you find that amusing?" Ivy asked.

"Seems like a big jump from the gambling saloons to land agent," Fargo said.

Ivy's brow furrowed. "Gambling saloons?"

"Ben Brewster was a gambling man last time I saw him. Worked the riverboats as well as the fancy saloons," Fargo said.

Ivy Evanston stared at him, shock wreathing her fine-featured, proper face. "I find that very hard to believe," she said.

"Believe it or not as you like. It happens to be true," Fargo said. "How'd you come to be his assistant?"

"Every land agent gets an assistant trained in keeping records. I was assigned to Ben," Ivy explained.

"Why didn't he come meet me himself?" Fargo asked.

"He's limping around on a bad sprain from when his horse fell in the mud," she said and gathered the reins in her hand. "I think we can go. They've finished their searching by now."

Fargo nodded and led the way from the little ravine, the Colt in his hand as he emerged from the trees, his ears straining for the sounds of horses. But he heard nothing and let Ivy lead the way west through the hackberry. The moon was past the midnight sky when she halted beneath a clump of peachleaf willow. "It's still a fair ride. I suggest we get some sleep and go on in the morning," Ivy said.

"Fine with me," Fargo agreed, swung from the saddle, and tossed his bedpack to the ground. He started to pull off clothes and saw that she took a moment to turn away and walk behind one of the broad, furrowed willow trunks. He was undressed down to his BVDs and lying on the bedroll when she reappeared in a shapeless, full-length nightgown that effectively cloaked her. She lay down on a blanket she spread near the trunk.

"Good night, Fargo," she said, her back to him, her voice crisp and businesslike. Ivy Evanston, he decided, was definitely not the type of woman that Ben Brewster used to have with him. But then it seemed that Ben was a new man. He found that hard to believe, also, Fargo mused. Men born with the gambling fever inside them, who enjoyed fleecing the less astute, seldom embraced the conventional life. He toyed with the thoughts as he let sleep come and slept heavily until the new sun woke him. He rose and saw Ivy Evanston sitting up, rubbing sleep from her eyes. He watched her rise from under the shapeless nightdress and go back behind the willow.

He used his canteen to wash and had just finished dressing when Ivy emerged, hair shiny and wet but carefully piled atop her head in her usual bun. In the daylight he saw that she had a trim figure under a dark green shirt and matching skirt, narrow hips and a tight rear that hardly moved as she walked, a bustline that seemed nicely balanced for the rest of her. Her face echoed her body, he decided, attractive in a very contained, disciplined way that just avoided being severe. "We should be at the cabin by midmorning," she said as she climbed onto her horse. "It's a small place we use as a central point."

"Central point for what?" Fargo queried.

"For setting up the land auctions," Ivy said. "Tell me, Fargo, did you and Ben meet at the gambling tables?"

"In a way. I was in a poker game with three crooked card sharps who tried to cheat me out of a winning hand. I called them on it, and they decided to shoot it out. I did in all three of them, but there was a fourth one standing by I didn't know about. He would have had me if Ben hadn't taken him out. I've owed Ben Brewster one ever since. It seems he's decided to call in that favor."

Ivy's brow held a small furrow. "Yes, I suppose that's about it. He told me he was sending for you because he needed someone with your talents, whatever they are," she said, regarding him thoughtfully.

"Some call me the Trailsman," Fargo said.

Ivy let her lips purse. "Yes, that would fit," she murmured.

"I'm a pretty good shot, too," Fargo said casually.

"That would also fit," she said.

"You want to fill me in on all this?" he asked.

"I'd rather Ben gave you the details," Ivy said. "It wouldn't be proper for me to do that."

"Doing what's proper important to you?" he questioned, a smile in his voice.

"Isn't it to you?" she returned, a hint of reproach in her glance.

"One for you," he conceded. "But I favor doing what's right more than what's proper."

"One for you," she said with a half nod.

Fargo rode beside her as she moved north through a stand of ironwood, onto lightly wooded terrain and finally across a line of low, open hills. At the bottom of the last hill a long, low-roofed cabin came into sight. Ben Brewster emerged as they reached the cabin, and Fargo saw he used a cane to help him walk.

"Fargo, it's good to see you," Ben Brewster called out. Fargo's eyes moved over the man and saw that Ben Brewster had put on a dozen or so pounds, his face a little jowly, his short-cropped hair and mustache touched with gray. But his bright blue eyes were as sharp as ever, tiny crinkles at the edges still able to fool people into thinking they were only casually observant. "I expected you two back yesterday," the man said.

"Unexpected delay," Fargo said, and when Ivy didn't elaborate, he gave a silent grunt. He liked that. She knew the value of being discreet. He followed Ben into the cabin and saw an interior divided into two rooms by a heavy drape, the nearest one holding an iron stove and a fireplace along with chairs and a cot.

"Sit down, old friend," Ben Brewster said as he eased himself into one of the heavy chairs.

"I'll put on coffee and make sandwiches," Ivy volunteered and went over to a puncheon table near the hearth.

"Guess you're wondering how I've come to be a government land agent," Ben Brewster said with a broad smile.

"Didn't figure it was hard work on your part," Fargo said blandly.

Ben Brewster laughed. "You always were a cynic, Fargo," the man said.

"With some people. I made an educated guess."

"And came up with what?"

"Somebody in a high place lost a powerful lot of money to you," Fargo said. "Enough to pay off with a job, his job, maybe."

Ben chuckled. "You always were smart, Fargo. But then you know me," he said.

"I just keep wondering what made you take it. What'd you see in it?" Fargo asked.

"I saw a great chance to turn over a new leaf, start a new life as an honest citizen," Ben Brewster said with a straight face.

"What else did you see in it?" Fargo tossed back.

"You're being cynical again," Ben said and managed to sound hurt.

"As you said, I know you," Fargo returned. "But I don't really give a rat's ass why you took it. I want to know why you've called in your chip."

Ben smiled. "Yes, of course," he said as Ivy came over with mugs of coffee and sandwiches. "Ivy's the perfect assistant. She's efficient, and she has a touch of the mother hen in her," Ben said. Fargo noted that Ivy didn't smile as she settled into a nearby chair, and Ben's eyes held on her for only a minute. "Been having trouble, Fargo," Ben said. "As land agent, I'm charged with offering government land at auction to the highest bidder. Remember, when statehood came in, damn near everything became government land."

"Including land that's been lived on?" Fargo inquired.

"Including. Everything goes up for auction unless somebody has filed a proper claim, and that's pretty much impossible seeing as how Washington wasn't taking claims for land until statehood. As land office agent, my job is to see that land auctions are held, that the highest bidder wins, and land ownership becomes registered and legal."

"So what's the trouble?" Fargo asked.

"Trouble is that buyers who've come looking to bid at an auction have suddenly left or plain disappeared," Ben Brewster said. "Some came to see me, and I haven't heard from them since. One or two auctions have been held, but the only bidders were already living on the land."

Fargo frowned into space. "That might explain why a group of masked riders took me by surprise and damn near beat me to death. They never said why, never said a damn thing."

"That sure fits what I've been suspecting. If somebody's scaring off bidders, I want them. I want names and faces I can put in jail. Right now all I have is a half dozen winning bids sent in at from a dollar to a dollar-and-a-quarter an acre. I can't believe there haven't been higher bids," Ben said.

"Don't *you* hold the auctions?"

"No. The law has a lot of dumb parts to it. As land office agent I call for the auctions, take and file the winning bids, but I don't hold the auctions. The law mandates that a respected member of the community serve as an auctioneer, some rot about wanting community involvement. The auctioneer is bound by law to take the highest bid, and I can't believe there haven't been higher bids than what I've seen. I know you can follow any damn kind of trail, and I can't hardly get around with this leg, so I sent for you."

"There's an auction to be held tomorrow night at a town called Highbridge in northwest Minnesota," Ivy put in.

"I know the place," Fargo said.

"I'm deputizing you to represent me," Ben said. "I want you at that auction to see what the hell's going on. I want to know how many outside bidders show up and what their bids were. Meanwhile, Ivy will be posting notices for another auction at a place called Bearsville in Deer Valley. She'll be finished by the time you report back to me."

"Good enough," Fargo said, finished the sandwich, and pushed to his feet.

"I'll see Fargo off," Ivy said to Ben. "The more you rest your leg the faster it'll heal."

"That's for sure," Ben grunted and settled back in his chair as Fargo walked from the cabin. Ivy halted beside him outside as he stopped at the Ovaro.

"You are a mother hen," Fargo remarked.

"No. I'm just trying to do my job," she said sharply.

He peered at her. "You're not too happy at your job, are you?" he questioned.

"I'm content," she said.

"That's not much of an answer."

"I was picked out of a pool of office assistants," she said. "I'll make the best of it."

"Maybe you're not happy being out here with Ben," he said, pressing her. "Ben's always had an eye for the ladies."

"Not for this one," she snapped.

"Maybe that's what's bothering you," he said and saw her eyes flash.

"Absolutely not. I meant that he needs an assistant, not a girlfriend. He's quite aware of that," Ivy said.

"That's nice," Fargo said blandly as he swung onto the horse. "See you soon." He rode away, then glanced back to see her still standing there. Maybe her prickly answers had been the truth, but they hadn't been all of it, Fargo mused as he rode on. There was something more, something that bothered her inside. He made a mental note to pursue that another time as he concentrated on making time on the smooth, long strides of the Ovaro.

4

The day had gone into the late afternoon when Fargo reached the northwest land, and he rode against a long line of red ash. When the trees curved downward into a hollow, he pulled back on the reins as a rider suddenly raced out of the trees and across the hollow. Three more riders came after him out of the trees, then another four farther up along the ash, their pursuit aimed at cutting off the fleeing horseman. Fargo's eyes grew narrow as he looked again at the pursuers. All wore hoods over their faces. He reined to a halt as they surrounded the one rider and knocked him to the ground.

Fargo reached back and pulled the big Henry from its saddle case. Maybe the hooded riders were the same ones who had almost beaten him to death, he reflected. Or maybe they were another group. It didn't much matter. They had the same objectives, apparently. The rifle at his shoulder, Fargo fired, and his first shot was a near miss. He corrected his aim, and at the second shot one of the hooded figures grabbed at his forearm. Fargo heard their shouts of surprise as they broke their circle and bolted for the trees. They became fleeting shapes inside the red ash, but he saw them start toward him. He fired off four more shots in a quick cluster, his object to dissuade rather than to bring down. He listened to the heavy rifle shells thud into tree trunks, heard another shout of pain, and saw the darting shapes change direction and flee back through the trees.

Two figures thought to linger and still come after him, but his next shot made them change their minds. He stayed in place as the band raced away through the forest until they were out of sight before he nosed the Ovaro into the hollow. The man they'd been chasing was just retrieving his horse that had run from him when he'd been pulled from the saddle. "Jesus, I sure owe you one, mister," the man said as Fargo rode to a halt. "Those bastards were going to kill me."

"Maybe," Fargo said.

"No maybe about it. They said so," the man answered.

"You know why?" Fargo questioned.

"I can make a damn good guess. I'm here for the land auction, came to town yesterday," the man said. "Seems they had other ideas. I'm just glad you were here."

"I'm from the land office," Fargo said and saw the man's eyes widen.

"Then you can give Ben Brewster a message. Tell him Sam Dodge is out. I like keeping my neck," the man snapped and climbed onto his horse, snapped the reins, and went into an instant gallop. The frown stayed on Fargo's brow as he walked the Ovaro forward. The man's words rode with him, curious words that left questions instead of explanations. Putting the pinto into a trot, Fargo rode west and took two unintentional detours on the way to the town of Highbridge. Both gave him a chance to see a half dozen pieces of developed land, mostly growing vegetables, but he noted two hog farms. He guessed there were more farms on the other side of town.

Night had fallen when he reached the sparse collection of buildings that made up the town. Lanterns lighted a long, open-sided structure that bore only a flat roof and, he guessed, served as a marketplace at other times. A small group of men and women were gathered under the roof, and nearly a dozen buckboards and one-horse farm wagons were parked outside. He drew to a halt at the end of the structure, and started to walk under the roof when he saw the young woman waiting in a dark green buckboard. His eyes held on the long blond hair first, then the slender figure in the blue dress with the smallish, high breasts. She turned, and he stared at the delicate, almost wan features of the face that combined shyness and sensuousness. The wave of surprise that struck him was almost physical, and he saw her eyes widening, her lips falling open as she saw him. He halted beside the buckboard, his eyes searching her face. "Waiting for somebody at the auction?" he asked softly.

Abby's lips worked, soundlessly at first, then her voice came, a strained whisper. "My father," she said. "What are you doing here, Fargo? You said you wouldn't come back."

"Never promised," Fargo said. The murmur of voices suddenly subsiding brought his attention to those gathered under the roof where a thin man in a black frock coat stepped onto a platform beside a crude lectern. "We'll talk later," Fargo said as he moved to stand at the edge of the crowd facing the lectern. The man's thin, lined face scanned the crowd and came to rest on Fargo.

"You here to bid or watch, mister?" he queried.

"Watch. I'm from the land office," Fargo said.

The man's brows lifted a fraction. "I'm Roy Hatchett, mayor of Highbridge. I've been asked to run this auction," he said and turned to his listeners. "Let's get started, folks. The first piece of land is one hundred acres with house, barn, stable, and corrals, worked by Len Cracket for the last eight years. Do I have a bid?"

"One dollar and twenty-five cents an acre," a man shouted and stepped forward.

The auctioneer's gavel came down instantly with a loud whack on the top of the lectern. "Sold to Len Cracket," he said, hardly drawing a breath before plunging ahead. "Next is a piece of prime land down by the river, seventy acres, two houses, two barns, worked by Hal Henderson. Do I hear a bid?"

"One dollar and twenty-five cents an acre," a man in a straw hat said as he waved his hand.

"Sold to Hal Henderson," the auctioneer said instantly as he banged his gavel. "Next is a fine piece of bottom land, just below Rock Ridge, good corn, lettuce, beets, everything a man can grow. Sixty acres with house and barn and silo. Worked for ten years by Chuck Hall. Give me a bid."

Fargo watched the man step forward, slight-built but tall, dark blond hair with a touch of gray, a face with the small, composed features that echoed Abby. "A dollar and a quarter an acre," Chuck Hall said.

Again the auctioneer's gavel banged down. "Sold," the man snapped and immediately went into his next offering. Fargo kept his face expressionless as every piece of land up for auction in the region was sold in the same manner at the same bidding price. Finally, the mayor brought his gavel down in a final thump.

"There being no further parcels of land up for auction and no further bidders, I call this auction over," the man said.

Fargo's jaw was tight as he slowly scanned the crowd, his eyes moving not from face to face but from waist to waist. His searching suddenly came to a halt as the heavy silver buckle with its distinctive molding seemed to throb in front of his eyes, a shape indelibly imprinted in his mind. Slowly, he brought his eyes upward, taking in a slight paunch that protruded over the top of the belt. But the chest above the belly was thick and powerful, the shoulders bull-like. Fargo's eyes went to the man's face, saw a thick-lipped mouth with a twist of cruelty in it, a wide nose and heavy, beetling brows. He saw the man peering back at him, recognition quickly masked as he looked away. Striking up a conversation with a man and a woman, the man turned his back on Fargo and began to walk away.

Fargo stepped quickly from under the roof to where the slender figure sat in the buckboard. Abby's eyes were round with concern as he halted beside her. "When?" Fargo muttered.

"I have to drive my father home. I can get away soon as he's asleep," Abby said.

"All right. There's something I have to do now. Where?" Fargo asked.

"The little cabin? Can you find it again?" Abby asked.

"I'll be there," Fargo said and strode to the Ovaro. He watched as Abby's father climbed into the buckboard beside her, and as they drove away his eyes sought out the man with the silver belt buckle. He found the thick-chested figure climbing onto a tall chestnut, and Fargo swung onto the Ovaro, waited, then watched the man ride away. He let the figure go out of sight in the darkness before he moved forward, and he hung back as he followed, letting his ears instead of his eyes guide his way. The pattern of the hoofbeats told him that the man had put his horse into a steady trot. Staying back, Fargo passed a field of open spaces studded with thick-leafed ironwood, continued to follow, and suddenly heard the hoofbeats slow ahead of him. The man was turning his horse, and, leaning from the saddle to peer at the ground, Fargo found where the man had turned a sharp right into a stand of wide ironwood.

Suddenly, there was only stillness, and, cursing under his breath, Fargo yanked the Ovaro to a halt, slid instantly from the saddle, and dropped low as he hit the ground. The shot came at once, grazing his shoulder as he rolled behind a tree trunk. He drew the Colt as he peered into the trees, then he rose on one knee and stayed motionless. Hardly breathing, he waited as a woodsman waits, listened as a hunter listens, and saw as a trailsman sees. Finally, the shadow came, a darker shape than the other shadows. It would have gone unnoticed by other men, but Fargo raised the Colt, waited, let the shadow become an amorphous shape. The shape moved again, took a step closer, and, aiming low, Fargo squeezed the trigger. He heard the sound he wanted to hear, a bullet smashing into metal, and he saw the six-gun sail into the air from beside the dark shape. "Goddamn," the man shouted, and Fargo darted from behind the tree, the Colt raised as the figure came forward.

"Son of a bitch," the man said. "Why are you following me?"

"You know why. That's not your real question. You

can't figure out how I knew," Fargo said, and the man's glowering silence was both an admission and an answer. "You should've worn a hood over your fancy silver belt buckle," Fargo said.

Surprise flooded the man's face for a moment, then turned into uncertain bravado. "All right, go on, shoot," the man said.

"That'd be too easy for you," Fargo said as he dropped the Colt into its holster. "It's payback time."

A snarling smile spread across the man's thick lips as he stepped forward. "You just made another mistake, mister," he said, long arms swinging loosely. Fargo rose on the balls of his feet, his lithe, muscular form poised to move in any direction. The man swung a long right, followed with a left, and crossed a right. Fargo easily ducked the blows, danced away, let the man come at him with another flurry of looping blows. The last one whistled past his cheek, and Fargo dropped into a crouch, his powerful shoulders knotting as he lashed out with a whistling left that landed on the man's jaw. His right followed instantly, landing at the same spot, and the man's head snapped backward. Fargo lifted a left hook and then a piledriver right into the man's midsection.

The man went down, rolled, then pushed to his feet again. But there was fear in his face as he came forward, Fargo saw, and felt satisfaction surge inside him. The man lunged as he threw a looping left and a right. Fargo blocked both blows, answered with a short uppercut, and a left dug hard into the man's stomach. As his blows landed, he felt the tearing pain of the whip lashing into his back as if it were happening that moment. His short right cross whistled forward with added rage, and he heard the man gasp in pain as one of his ribs cracked. Fargo's left caught the man as he was on his way down, spun him around, and he landed on his face. Fargo waited as the man took a moment to push to his feet, turn, and now his mouth hung open, blood coursing down the side of his jaw, his body bent forward with the pain of his broken rib. "Too bad you don't have your whip or your friends with you now," Fargo flung at him as he waited, let the man come forward, and met a wild left with his own short, jolting blow.

The man staggered and swayed. Fargo's right, delivered with all his strength, landed on the point of the man's jaw. He felt the man's jaw break as the thick-chested figure seemed to deflate. The man took a single step backward before he crashed to the ground and lay gasping between groans, tried to raise his head, and failed. He lay on his back, his body quivering with pain, and Fargo lowered his arms. "Account closed," he murmured as he turned away and climbed onto the Ovaro. He rode without glancing back, moved unhurriedly through the night, and searched for the signs that finally brought him to the little line cabin beside the pond.

She was there, a lamp burning low inside the cabin, and he dismounted and pushed the door open. He pulled his hand from the butt of the Colt as he entered, swearing at himself for letting distrust grow so quickly. Abby's eyes searched his face and found only hardness in the line of his jaw. "I settled with the one who did the whipping," Fargo said grimly. "Your pa was one of the others, wasn't he?" Pain came into her eyes as she nodded. "That what made you an angel of mercy? A big dose of guilt?" he insisted.

"Only at first," she said. "The rest was you and I. You have to know that. I'm not that good an actress."

"You could have told me, at least later," he said.

"I was afraid," she said.

"Afraid or ashamed?"

"Both," Abby murmured. "I know what they've been doing is wrong, but it's not that simple. You have to understand."

"I'm listening," Fargo said.

"There was nothing here when my pa and the others settled their lands, no government, no claims office, nothing. They staked their claims, lived on their lands. Everybody's claim was set down in detail, all proper boundaries recorded, titles and owners listed, everything registered. Settlers all over the territory organized claims clubs to keep records and be ready to file proper claims when the time came. My pa's the recorder for our club. And then the territory became a state."

"Government, what you wanted," Fargo said.

"But not the way it's happened. The government's come along with land auctions. It doesn't make any difference if the land has been worked for years. They say we're squatters, homesteaders, and anyone can come in with a high bid and buy the land."

"So these claims clubs have decided to make their own rules," Fargo said.

"For self-protection. Their records will stand up in any court," Abby said.

"Only the bids have all been rigged, no outside buyer has a chance. They appoint an auctioneer who freezes out any other bidders they haven't killed or driven away. The government land offices won't accept claims made without free bidding," Fargo said.

"They'll take their chances on that," Abby said.

"They've killed and beaten people to stop bids. They can't go on doing that. They'll be seen as criminals, not just squatters."

"There's no proof of that. The bids have been accepted and will be filed with the land office," Abby said.

"Meanwhile, they'll keep on killing and terrorizing?" Fargo said and saw the pain in Abby's eyes. "They can't go on with that."

"Don't you see that bidders with money will outbid everyone who's worked the land for years. That's all wrong," Abby protested.

"So's what they're doing. Two wrongs don't make a right," Fargo said. "This has to be stopped."

"Will you stop it, Fargo?" she asked almost tearfully.

"I mightn't have a choice," Fargo told her.

She stepped forward, and pressed her palms against his chest. "There's always a choice," she said.

"You'd have me say nothing, do nothing?" Fargo frowned.

"Let things take their own course," Abby said.

"Just forget about what they've done?" he pressed.

"They've been forced into protecting what's rightfully theirs."

"Nobody's forced into wearing hoods and killing," Fargo said.

"What would you have them do?" she threw back.

"Take their case to the government."

"They went to the land office agent, a Mr. Ben Brewster. He told them that under the law they were like any other bidders for land, and he had to enforce the law," Abby said. "They felt the cards were stacked against them."

Fargo grimaced inwardly. He could understand, even sympathize with those who saw everything they'd worked for taken from them. Bad laws bring bad results. "I think there'll have to be some reckoning for what they've done, but I'll talk to Ben Brewster. Maybe there's some way out of this," he said.

Abby's arms came up and encircled his neck. "Meanwhile there's now," she murmured. "This is a found moment, just like that first time was a found moment, unplanned, unexpected." Her lips came onto his, lightly first, then pressing, her mouth opening, hungering. "Found moments should never be wasted," she said.

"Never," he said as his fingers opened buttons. She was on the cot with him in moments, her flesh against his, and he again enjoyed the smallish breasts, the delicately pink little nipples that were so right on her half girl, half woman, wood nymph body. Her small, almost frantic cries of pleasure, the slender, wan figure that could be so unexpectedly sensuous, all returned as she made love to him. But there was something different, he realized dimly as he moved inside her and felt her gasping ecstasy, a kind of desperation, an urgency that went beyond the senses. But passion clouded reflection for Fargo as Abby writhed, rubbed her little triangle up and down against his body, pushing her pubic mound hard into his muscled frame, and as she did, her every motion excitingly sinuous. He matched her urgent demands and brought her gasping eagerness to new heights until his pulsating erectness exploded within her and her half screams gasped into the night, finally to trail away, leaving only soft murmurings.

She lay beside him, drawing in deep breaths until she finally sat up, smallish breasts hardly moving, and he saw a tiny furrow crease her brow as she peered at him. "It wasn't the same," she said, sadness more than disappointment in her voice.

He studied her for a moment. "You've just learned something," he said gently. "It wasn't the same because you weren't the same."

"The magic was missing," she murmured.

"Because the magic is in what you bring, not what you do," he said. She thought over his words in silence as she reached for clothes. He rose, dressed, and her hand held his as they walked from the cabin.

"You going to try?" she asked, no added words necessary.

"Yes," he said. "I have to report what I've seen and what I know. Maybe I can find some way around it. I don't know."

"Try," Abby murmured, her head against his chest. "For me. For that first time." She stepped back quickly, and he didn't answer as he swung onto the Ovaro. She watched as he rode away.

When he was deep in the ironwood, he knew there was no easy answer inside him. Perhaps it was wrong to try to find one, he pondered. There had been killings, and killings weren't acts to go unpunished. Maybe the guilty could plead extenuating circumstances. In the right climate before the right judge, they might find mercy. But those decisions would belong to others, and he was glad for it, Fargo grunted inwardly.

He reached a ridge where a line of bur oak grew, reined to a halt, and took down his bedroll. He slept quickly, glad to hide away from the search for answers that brought only more questions.

5

Ben Brewster came to the door with his cane as Fargo rode to a halt in the morning sunlight. "Come inside," Ben said, and Fargo followed him into the cabin to see Ivy at the table with a stack of forms in front of her. "Ivy thought it'd be proper to have claim forms all ready for the high bidders to fill out," Ben said. "What'd you find out?"

"Nothing you'll like hearing," Fargo said and proceeded to tell Ben everything he had seen for himself and learned from Abby.

"I was right," Ben growled when Fargo finished. "Bring the sonofabitches in, one by one if you have to. Start with the girl's pa as he's recording secretary for their club."

"They'll deny everything. We've no hard proof to make arrests. Knowing's one thing. Proving's another," Fargo said.

"Then get the proof. Beat it out of somebody," Ben Brewster snarled.

"That wouldn't be any more right than what they've been doing," Ivy put in.

"I don't need opinions from assistants," Ben snapped, and Fargo saw Ivy's face grow red, her jaw tighten as she looked down at the table. "Get the proof, arrest the bastards, and we'll take their lands," Ben said.

"That might be easier said than done," Fargo suggested.

"For most men, not for you," Ben Brewster said.

"Maybe we can make part of this a little easier," Fargo said. "We'll tell them their claims won't be accepted unless they stop what they've been doing and hold another auction—a proper, open one. That'll be a start. We can prefer charges later."

"Screw that. Get proof and arrest the whole goddamn bunch of them," Ben flung back. "I want you at the auction in Deer Valley tomorrow. See if the same thing's going on there. Take Ivy. She knows where it'll be held."

Brewster was in no mood to entertain any compromise, and Fargo decided to see if time and second thoughts might soften his stand. "It's your call," he said and glanced at Ivy. "Get your things and we'll leave," he said. She rose and went into the other half of the cabin, a touch of red still clinging to her cheeks, he noticed. He took the moment to turn to Ben, again.

"Met a man named Sam Dodge, saved his neck for him. He said to tell you he was out. What'd he mean by that?" Fargo queried.

"I guess he meant he wasn't going to bid. Can't say I blame him," Brewster said.

"Why tell you?" Fargo queried.

"He stopped at the office a week ago. Guess he just wanted me to know what he decided," Brewster said.

"Still seems a strange way of putting it," Fargo said.

"Not to me," Brewster said, and Fargo turned away with a half shrug. There was something more, he was certain. It had been in Brewster's eyes, a brief moment of alarm at the message. Striding from the cabin, he was waiting outside when Ivy came out with her saddlebag, her face set, and he watched her climb onto the horse. "Get back soon as you can. I want to know what's going on," Ben called from inside the cabin as Fargo moved the Ovaro forward.

Ivy set a fast pace north through easy riding country brilliant with golden aspen. She rode in silence, and when the day began to slide into dusk, he pointed to a ridge where the trees formed a natural barrier to the night winds. She nodded and followed him as he climbed to the ridge line and dismounted.

"What's pulling at you?" he asked as they unsaddled the horses and put down blankets and bedrolls.

"Nothing," she said.

"Didn't your mother teach you not to lie?" he said blandly. She shot him a quick glower.

"Just because I don't chatter on when I ride?" she tossed back.

"There's being quiet, and there's being wrapped in dark clouds," he commented.

The glower softened, more unhappy than angry. "I don't think I ought to talk about it," she said.

"Why not?" Fargo questioned.

"I was raised to believe in loyalty. I'm Ben Brewster's assistant. I owe him my loyalty, not my opinions," Ivy said.

"Try your opinions on me. I'm interested in them," Fargo said as dusk settled quickly over the ridge.

She peered at him, a furrow pressing into her brow. "I know those homesteaders have done wrong," she said. "But I can't help feeling sorry for them. Everything they've built could be bought out from under them. It doesn't seem fair. I wish he'd taken your suggestion."

"He didn't, and it's his call," Fargo said.

"So it is," she agreed.

"Anything else you want to tell me?" he probed.

She hesitated, then shook her head. "It's not my place. I feel disloyal saying what I have," she said, turned away, and took two beef jerky strips from her saddlebag and folded herself on the blanket with them. He wouldn't press her further, not for now, he decided. Loyalty was a quality he couldn't fault, and he sat down on his bedroll with his own pemmican and jerky strips. The night was black when they finished eating, and she rose, went behind a wide-trunked aspen to change, and came back in the shapeless nightgown that covered her too well. She started to move her blanket farther from his bedroll when he stopped her.

"Leave it there," he said, and she frowned at him. "I don't want you off on your own."

"You afraid of something?" she questioned.

"We wouldn't be the only critters attracted by this ridge. It affords a great view and wind shelter," he said as the moon began to rise and cast its pale light on the land below. Ivy left the blanket alone and settled down, turning her back on him as he undressed to near nakedness.

"Good night," she said over her shoulder.

"'Night," he answered, staying a moment on one elbow and watching her lay with her arms crossed over her breasts, hair still pulled back atop her head in a bun. It was a statement, he realized and smiled, a proper formality even as she slept. He turned on his side. The day had been a hard ride, then the brief turn-around, and back in the saddle. He felt tiredness pull on him, closed his eyes, and was deep in sleep in moments. He slept heavily, and the moon was moving across the distant sky when his eyes snapped open. The sound had cut through his sleep, and he knew it at once as he came awake, the unmistakable half snarl and half cry of a cougar. He sat up, his glance going to the blanket alongside him at once. It was empty.

He rolled over and yanked the Colt from its holster on the bedroll beside him as the cougar's hissing cry came again. Coming up on his feet, he moved forward in a crouch, his eyes sweeping the ridge in the last light of the moon. He saw her after a moment, shrinking back along the ground just below the top line of the ridge. The cougar's long, low form came into sight as the big cat moved toward Ivy, slinking forward, body lowered, poised to attack. Fargo raised the Colt, fired, and saw his shot thud into the ground a fraction of an inch in front of the cougar. The big cat reacted instantly, leaping backward, twisting its sleek body in midair. It hit the ground and became a dark streak fleeing down the side of the ridge, surprise and self-preservation guiding its reaction.

Fargo's eyes went to Ivy and saw fear still frozen in her face as she half fell, half leaped into his arms. She clung to him, trembling, and he felt the softness of her inside the nightgown. "What the hell were you doing out here?" he growled.

"I woke up. I couldn't get back to sleep," she said, still clinging to him. "I decided to sit and look down over the ridge."

"Why couldn't you sleep?" he asked as she stopped trembling and pulled back.

"I don't know," she said.

"You're getting real good at real bad answers," he said. Her face tightened for a moment, then softened, and her arms came up to slide around his neck.

"Thank you for being there. I could have been killed," she said. Her lips touched his, tentative, unsure, but very soft, stayed only a moment, and then drew back. Her brown eyes mirrored the uncertainty of her lips as she struggled with feelings.

"Relax," he said softly. "You said your thanks. That's enough."

She blinked back. "I'm new at this." she said.

"At kissing?" he asked, one brow lifting.

She gave a sheepish half smile. "Pretty new," she said. "But I meant at being grateful, at having my life saved. I have to sort out what I'm feeling."

He took her arm as he climbed to the trees with her. "Stay near while you're sorting," he said.

"Yes, definitely," she said, and her arm tightened around his, and he felt the soft side of her breast through the nightgown. He kept his arm there until they reached the trees and she sat on the blanket. "I have to sort out everything about this land," she said.

"It won't be easy. This is a land that brings out the worst and the best in people," he said.

"I'm learning that," she said, and he felt her eyes moving up and down his muscled body as he stretched out. She turned on her side, her back to him, and he heard her deep sigh as she cradled herself once more. He closed his eyes and let himself sleep. Ivy would do her own sorting in her own way, he was certain. As with that streak of loyalty inside her, she'd neither accept nor discard things lightly. The moon neared the dark horizon as he slept, and he woke only when the sun bathed his face with its yellow warmth.

He sat up, and saw Ivy stir, push up on her elbows, and look across at him. She still managed to look proper, he noted with an inward smile, hardly a hair out of place in the bun on top of her head. He pulled on clothes as she dressed behind the tree and had the horses saddled when she emerged. "There's a lake the other side of the ridge," he said. "You can bathe there."

"How do you know?" She frowned.

He pointed to a swarm of goldfinch, their yellow bodies contrasting in the sun with their black fore-heads and wings as they soared down the far side of the ridge. "Birds fly to water in the morning, away from it in the evening. We just follow," he said and swung onto the Ovaro. The lake came into view at the base of a low dip in the land, a small, irregular-shaped body of clear blue water nestled behind a line of gran-ite rocks. The goldfinch didn't stop their swooping and chattering as Fargo and Ivy rode to a halt, and Fargo nodded in satisfaction. It was another sign. The birds would pick up anything with the feel of danger and take wing at once, an instinctive thing, the inner wisdom of all wild things.

"You first," Fargo said as he swung from the pinto. "I'll stay here behind the rocks."

She slid from her horse and took a towel from her saddlebag. "Can I trust you to be a gentleman?" she asked.

"Ordinarily no," he said. "But I'll make an excep-tion for you."

"Thank you," she said.

"I yell, you come, whether you're buck naked or not, understand?" he said.

"Understand," she said and hurried out of sight past

the rocks. He leaned against a low rock, and his eyes scanned the aspen and the tall rocks that almost surrounded the lake. It was still Osage, Dakota, Iowa, and Ojibwa country. But mostly he watched the goldfinch and enjoyed their winged patterns. Nothing disturbed their swooping and fluttering, no sudden flights of alarm, and finally Ivy returned, looking scrubbed and dried. Her hair was back in the bun, but held a fresh, wet sheen. He took his own towel and started for the lake, then paused to glance back.

"Can I trust you to be a lady?" he asked blandly.

She didn't smile. "Of course," she said. "But it'll be difficult."

He glanced again at her, his eyebrows lifting. "That's a kind of compliment," he said.

"It's honesty. Settle for that," she said with a touch of asperity. He walked on to the lake, shed clothes, and plunged into the cool water, washed the road dust from his body, and rubbed himself dry when he emerged. Dressed, he climbed around the rocks to see Ivy sitting beside the horses, her face quietly tensed.

"Still sorting?" he asked as she rose and climbed onto her horse.

"Yes," she said and swung beside him as he sent the Ovaro from the lake. She rode lead when they reached the forested terrain and led the way through a stand of red ash. The sun was nearing the noon sky, and they were crossing open land made of hollows and rises when, directly in their path, he saw the slowly circling forms in the sky, their black, huge wings tracing an indolent path. One floated lazily downward to disappear behind a cluster of high brush while another rose in flight, its featherless, naked red head cronelike with wrinkles.

"Buzzards," Fargo muttered.

"Something's dead out there?" Ivy frowned.

"Count on it," Fargo said. "You stay here." She nodded gratefully, and he spurred the pinto forward and pushed through the tall, dry brush. Four of the big black birds were on the ground, clustered around an object that, as he rode closer, took shape as the body of a man. The buzzards merely glanced up at him as they continued pulling flesh from the body, their powerful bills tearing away clothing. He dismounted, strode forward, and waved his hat. Reluctantly, hardly bothered, the buzzards backed away and took wing, except for one that remained on the ground with a disdainful glare. Fargo halted beside the figure, grimacing at the sight and the sharp yet cloying odor.

There was little left distinguishable of the man's face but Fargo's eyes grew narrow as he slowly scanned the body. Along with the gouged and torn flesh of the chest, Fargo saw a jagged hole and a wide line of dried blood, a wound not made by sharp beaks but by a bullet. Forcing himself to fight off the odor of death and decay, he went through the pockets of the man's jacket, pulled out a folded piece of paper, and backed away to read the few lines scrawled on it.

Johnson—

All you have to do is come in high bidder and bring me the final bid signed by the auctioneer. I take care of everything else.

Ben Brewster

Fargo frowned down at the note, pushed it into his pocket, and pulled himself onto the Ovaro. He left the grisly scene, and the big black buzzards swooped back immediately. Ivy, her eyes round, filled with unsaid questions, waited for him to halt beside her. "Another bidder who never got to bid," Fargo said.

Ivy's lips tightened. "The same attackers?" she asked.

"Doubt it. Not their territory," Fargo said.

"Then you think all the claims clubs are into it," she said.

"I'll tell you after the next auction, but I don't like it," he said. "I'm going on alone. I want you to go back to your office."

She thought for a moment. "I'm not afraid," she said.

"Good for you. Now get started back," he said. "I'll find the place."

"Stay north. You'll see the valley. The town's at the end of it, an open shed where they'll hold the auction," Ivy said, and her hand came to touch his. "Be careful, please."

"Always. I'm just an observer," he said with a smile she didn't return. He slapped her horse on the rump and sent it cantering away, turned the Ovaro, and rode on. He held a steady pace, but the day was nearly at an end when he reached the valley and finally the town. He found the large open shed where wagons and horses were already gathered. He dismounted and stood at one side, aware of instant glances, all suspicious, some outrightly hostile. More wagons arrived, men and women climbing from them, and a portly man with silver gray hair climbed onto a platform.

"I'm honored you've picked me to run this here auction," he said, and his eyes turned to Fargo. "I'm

Pastor Freed, First Methodist Church. Who might you be, mister?"

"Name's Fargo. I'm here from the land office," Fargo said.

"The land office agent's named Ben Brewster," a voice said from the crowd.

"That's right. He sent me," Fargo said, his eyes going to the platform. "Didn't expect a preacher to be running the auction," he commented.

"The good people of Deer Valley wanted to be sure a right and honest auction was held," the man said and turned his attention to the crowd in front of him. "This here auction is hereby open. First piece of land is a hundred twenty acres worked and farmed by Ed Snavely. Let's hear a bid."

A thin man in worn clothes rose and raised his hand. "One dollar and ten cents an acre," he said.

The preacher clapped his hands together. "Sold to Ed Snavely," he said instantly, and a round of applause followed. Fargo kept his face expressionless as the pastor called out another piece of land. Keeping his place, Fargo watched the charade unfold exactly as it had in Highbridge. The pastor's ideas of a right and proper auction had been tailor-made for his flock, and Fargo wondered how much else the man knew. Maybe he was only a willing dupe. It didn't really matter. What mattered was that the claims clubs were all bent on the same ruthless self-protection. Perhaps Ben Brewster was right, Fargo reflected. Things had all gone too far, actions and attitudes that destroyed reason and compromise. He was still stone-faced when the auction ended and the preacher came to him. "I'll be sending Mr. Brewster the properly stamped paperwork with the winning bids," he said.

Fargo thought of telling the man the results wouldn't be accepted, but decided it'd serve no purpose. "You do that," he said and strode away. When he rode into the night, he felt a terrible sadness at the headlong pace of events. They seemed beyond stopping, the good turned bad, new laws that brought injustice instead of justice, everything right being done for the wrong reasons. And a former riverboat gambler as land office agent, the upholder of the law. It somehow fitted a time and place where everything seemed upside down. He rode with his thoughts till the moon crossed the midnight sky, slept under the thick green husks of a black walnut, then continued on when the new day came.

He was nearing the land that led to Ben Brewster's office cabin when he heard it, that low rumbling of hooves and throaty bellows mingled together to create the special sound common to all cattle herds. He crossed over a low rise to find his way blocked by an expanse of longhorns, some three hundred, he estimated. He saw eight or so cowhands riding the fringes of the herd and found wagons rolling slowly along behind the cattle, one a chuck wagon, the others three canvas-topped, high-sided Kansas freight wagons. He made his way around the slow-moving mass of longhorns as the cowhands brought the herd to a halt. When he reached the last of the wagons, he immediately recognized the figure that stepped from the rear, the gold watch fob hanging from the vest, the coarse-featured face, flattened nose, and balding head.

"Well, well, it's Fargo," Burt Davis said. "Been waiting for you to get back." Fargo's eyes went past the man as Lila Davis swung from the wagon, her face sullen as she stared at him, hands on her hips with a kind of belligerent provocativeness. "I still want you to break trail for me, Fargo," Burt Davis said. Fargo's eyes returned to Lila.

"I'd say that's not a majority opinion," he commented.

Burt Davis chuckled. "It's the only opinion that counts," he said. "Lila holds grudges. She'll come around."

"But I won't," Fargo said. "I still have a job," Fargo said.

"Not anymore you don't," Burt Davis said, and Fargo frowned at the man. "There's nothing to stop you from breaking trail for me."

Fargo was still frowning at Burt Davis when the voice broke in. "He's right. You're dismissed," it said, and Fargo saw Ben Brewster come around the rear of the wagon. "I'm not land office agent anymore. I quit," Ben said. "Joined up with Burt."

"Just like that?" Fargo frowned.

"Decided it was getting too dangerous. Never did like it much, anyway," Ben Brewster said.

"What about Ivy?" Fargo inquired.

"She's got the job. I officially turned it over to her before I quit. She's back at the cabin," Ben said.

"Jesus," Fargo bit out. "You just walked out on her."

"I wouldn't put it that way. I promoted her," Ben demurred.

"Goddamn, you're a piece of work," Fargo said, fished into his pocket, and brought out the note, then thrust it at the man. "Found this note in the pocket of another bidder who never made it. You want to explain it to me?"

"What's to explain?" Ben said evenly as he read the note.

"Sounds like you were working with him," Fargo said.

"Nonsense. Johnson wrote me for information on how the auctions worked. I wrote him that note explaining the procedure," Brewster said, handing the note back. Fargo said nothing further on it. The explanation had been reasonable enough, perhaps too reasonable when coupled with the message from the other man. Or was he being unfair? Fargo asked himself. Was he letting Ben's past color his thinking? He grimaced inwardly and remained unsatisfied as he pocketed the note.

"You can start in the morning, Fargo. Same offer. I'm sure you remember how generous it was," Burt Davis put in.

"I remember," Fargo said, letting his eyes sweep the herd. "Seems to me you've got help."

"All cowhands, none of them trailsmen. I still need someone to break trail. Hell, you've no reason to turn down all that money, now," Burt Davis said.

"Doesn't seem so," Fargo conceded. "I want to pay Ivy a visit, first," Fargo said.

"We'll camp here for the night," Burt Davis said, and Fargo cast a glance at Lila. She still glowered, but her eyes hadn't left him, he noted as he sent the pinto forward. He rode south at a fast canter and daylight still clung to the land when he reached the cabin. Ivy came out, hurrying to him as he dismounted, anxiety in her face.

"I heard," he said.

"And I'm still in shock," Ivy said. "I don't understand how he could just up and do this."

"Exactly what happened?" Fargo questioned.

"Ben was nervous waiting for you to get back. I was finishing some forms when the Davises came along with their herd. Ben went outside, talked to them most of the morning, then came back and told me he was quitting. I was speechless."

"I'll bet," Fargo grunted. "He promoted you into the job."

"Into something I'm not able to do," Ivy said.

"You could hang on," Fargo said.

"Absolutely not," Ivy snapped. "I wouldn't know how to handle whatever problems came up. I was hired as an assistant, nothing more. I'm going back. I was hoping you would help me."

Fargo frowned into space for a moment. "Burt Davis is still offering a lot of money for me to break trail for him," he said.

Reproach mixed with disbelief flooded Ivy's face. "You're not going to take it, are you?"

"I just might," Fargo said.

"With that wife of his along? My God, I don't believe this. I thought you had some principles," Ivy exploded. "It seems I was wrong."

"Now, you just simmer down," Fargo said. "There's something very wrong about all this, about Ben, about his relationship with some of the bidders, and now this sudden decision to quit. It doesn't add up. The Davises' cattle drive doesn't add up, either."

"What's wrong about that?" Ivy asked.

"There's no sense in driving cattle across territory where there are no stock buyers, no markets, no shipping depots, and nowhere to ship. And now Ben's suddenly getting together with them. Nothing adds up right. If I break trail for them, maybe I'll have a chance to find out what's going on."

"It's over here. Any bids that come in are invalid. We know that now. They're going to have to find a better way to hold land auctions. I'm going back. I'll find my way to Duncan's Corners. There might be a weekly stage there," Ivy said.

"There's an awful lot of wild territory between here and Duncan's Corners," Fargo said. "Have you enough food to hole up here?"

"For a little while."

"I want a chance to see what I can find out, and then I'll come back for you," Fargo said. Ivy looked dubious, and he didn't blame her. "Give me a week," he said.

"I don't know," she said. "You do what you have to do. I'll think about it."

"I'll come back for you," he said, hands pressing into her shoulders.

Her eyes, darkly serious, searched his face. "Promise?" she murmured.

"Promise," he said. Her lips were parted, but a few inches from his, and she took a half step forward, paused, her breath a soft half gasp and, pulling her lips closed, she stepped back. "It's hard to stay proper," he said softly.

"Be careful," Ivy breathed as she turned and hurried into the cabin as dusk slid into night. He rode away slowly, found a cluster of box elder, and settled onto his bedroll, softly swearing at the realization that there'd be no easy way to ferret out the truth. Ben Brewster was too good a poker player to let much slip, and liquor made Burt Davis pass out before it loosened his tongue. Lila swam into his thoughts. Her anger and her hunger could be used. She might turn out to be the most vulnerable, he concluded, then closed his eyes and slept till the morning sun woke him.

6

Fargo saw they were preparing to move when he reached the herd, Burt Davis holding the reins of the largest wagon, Ben sitting beside him. "You've a deal," Fargo said and Davis gave a wide grin.

"Now you're being smart," he said, swung from the wagon, and led him to where the cowhands were emptying coffeepots. "This is Jack Bansen, my trail foreman," Davis introduced, halting before a heavyset man with a bristly mustache. Fargo exchanged nods with Jack Bansen and the others, quickly taking in the eight men with the Trailsman's eyes that probed where others only looked. They were a hard-bitten lot with tight mouths and cold eyes, none of the comfortable casualness of cowhands in them, he noted. Returning to Burt's wagon, he climbed onto the Ovaro as Ben spoke up.

"How was Ivy?" Ben asked.

"She's staying for the moment," Fargo said.

"She have anything else to say to you?" Ben asked with studied casualness.

"Such as?" Fargo returned.

"Anything, what she's thinking, how she feels?" Ben said.

"Not much, but I wouldn't say she's happy," Fargo

told him. Ben nodded, but Fargo caught an uneasiness in the man's face.

Turning, Fargo waved an arm at the cowhands alongside the herd. "Let's move 'em out," he called and slowly rode past the herd, skirting the long, hooked horns that could disembowel a man with the toss of a head. He led the way north along land with flat, open high plains, rode on alone to see that the plains stayed open with only a few clusters of box elder that posed no problems. The sun was past the noon sky when the town came into view, a dozen small buildings and a sign that proclaimed itself Deer Plains. He passed a saloon, a number of grain sheds, the town dotted with hay wagons and Owensboro one-horse farm wagons. He pulled to a halt before a man wearing a sheriff's badge and puffing on a long cigar.

"Any water near here?" he asked. "Name's Fargo. Got a herd of longhorns coming along."

"Fargo? The one they call the Trailsman?" the sheriff asked.

"Guilty," Fargo said.

"Never saw a big herd driven up this way. Where in hell you taking them?" the sheriff said.

"The boss hasn't made up his mind yet. He's a man who likes to pioneer," Fargo said.

"Addison's Creek runs for some three miles north," the sheriff said.

"Much obliged. I'll see the herd gives you plenty of room," Fargo said, turned the Ovaro, and rode back to the slow-moving herd. Lila rode a big gray alongside the wagon with Burt and Ben Brewster in the driver's seat. "There's a town up ahead," Fargo said.

"You talk to anyone there?" Burt asked.

"The sheriff," Fargo said.

"He know who you were?" Burt queried.

"Matter of fact, he did. Why?" Fargo frowned.

"Don't want him to think we're a bunch of no-bodies driving a herd up this way," Burt said with a satisfied smile.

Fargo called to Jack Bansen, "Keep to the left. We don't want to be driving those longhorns through the town," he said. Bansen nodded and rode off to follow his orders.

"I'll pick you up on the other side of town," Fargo said and sent the Ovaro on. He had left sight of the herd when hoofbeats came to his ears, and he turned in the saddle to see Lila on the big gray.

"I want to talk," she said as she drew to a halt and slid from the horse, deep breasts bouncing inside a white shirt. Fargo dismounted and faced her heavy-lidded eyes that still held anger. "You're going to make up for what you did," Lila muttered.

"You mean for what I didn't do," Fargo corrected, and her eyes suddenly flashed ice.

"Don't be smart with me, damn you," she hissed. "I'll find the time and the place. Just you be ready. Any more stunts and you're a dead man, I promise you."

"That's not very romantic," Fargo said mildly.

"You know what I want, and romance has nothing to do with it," Lila said.

"You're right about that. How about what I want?" he said.

"What's that?" She frowned.

"Tell me how Burt and you met Ben?" he asked.

"It just happened," she said. "Fate, maybe." He smiled and saw the mask slide over her eyes.

"Fate. Can't argue with that," he said. She was lying, of course, he knew. It was in her eyes, but lies can be revealing. One question had been answered. Ben Brewster hadn't just quit because things were getting dangerous. He hadn't joined up with Burt Davis on an impulse. There was a connection, somehow, someway. Fate hadn't a damn thing to do with it. He watched Lila climb onto the big gray and waved at her as she rode off. It had been a beginning. He'd find his way to the rest.

He swung onto the Ovaro and rode north until he was opposite the town. He waited till the herd appeared, then watched the longhorns pass by without problems, staying back as the herd moved on. Burt and Ben drew up behind in the last wagon, Lila riding alongside them, and he saw her cast a glance his way. No glower in it now. She was satisfied she had made her point.

The longhorns were almost out of sight when Fargo saw a lone rider galloping toward him. The last of the afternoon sun caught the long blond hair, and he rode to meet her, seeing the pain in her face as she skidded the horse to a stop. "My father," she gasped out. "They killed him, last night. Len Crocket, too."

"Who killed him?" Fargo questioned.

"Men, six at least. They wore kerchiefs over their faces. We were all asleep when they came. I managed to hide," Abby said.

"They just came killing for no reason?"

"Oh, they had a reason. They took the metal lock boxes that held all the winning bids and property forms. Pa had them as secretary of our claims club," she said. "He tried to fight them off, but they killed him, damn near killed Ma, too."

"Chickens coming home to roost," Fargo said.

"That's a rotten thing to say," Abby protested.

"It is, but it's also the truth," he answered. "How'd you find me?"

"I went to Ben Brewster. The woman there said he wasn't in and you were leading a cattle drive," Abby said.

"Why'd you go looking for Brewster?" Fargo asked.

"To tell him to call off his land auctions. There was no trouble till he came with his auction notices. That started every terrible thing that's happened."

"Most of it done by your claims clubs," Fargo reminded her.

"They didn't do this," she flung back at him.

"You don't know that," he said.

"No, that's impossible," she said.

"I'll admit it's not likely," Fargo conceded. "Anyway, Ben Brewster quit. He's no longer land office agent. That young woman is for now, Ivy Evanston."

"Then she can call off the auctions," Abby said.

"Only Washington can do that," Fargo said.

"She's here. She can stop them," Abby insisted.

Fargo thought for a moment. Maybe it might be the best thing, he mused. "I'll talk to her," he said. "You go home. I'm sorry about your pa. I'll see if I can get hold of anything."

"Anything. I want to know anything you hear," Abby said and sent her horse into a fast canter, blond hair still catching the last of the sun on the horizon now. He felt sorry for her. She'd been caught up in something she never really believed in, but now grief, loyalty, and anger had hardened her, emotions capable of doing just that. He put the Ovaro into a gentle trot as thoughts raced through his mind. Was there a traitor within one of the claims clubs, someone out to take advantage of turmoil and confusion? Or was there a new opportunist with his own agenda? Did Ben Brewster really quit because he was suddenly afraid? Was Burt Davis just doing his own thing? Suddenly, everything was changed. Or was it? Fargo swore as he caught up to where the herd had halted for the night.

Ben, Burt Davis, and Lila were finishing a meal before a small fire. He didn't dismount. He wanted to turn off any thoughts Lila might be harboring about the night. "I'll be back come morning," he said.

"Where are you going?" Burt Davis frowned.

"I like exploring by night when there's a good moon. Fewer things to watch out for, fewer distractions, just me and the trails," Fargo said. It was only a partial lie. "There's been trouble," he said to Ben and told him of Abby's visit.

"No shit," Ben grunted. "Serves the bastards right."

Fargo shrugged, the man's reaction normal enough. "No matter to you anymore, right?" Fargo said.

"Right. Not one damn bit," Ben said, and Fargo moved the Ovaro forward, ignored Lila's eyes, and rode slowly past the cattle. He listened to the clicking sound of horns hitting against horns and noted that most of the cowhands were around the chuck wagon with only a few at the edges of the herd. He rode on, and a three-quarter moon came up to light his way across the high plain. The land stayed wide and flat, and he'd ridden well into the night when he saw the plains divide, one half staying high and straight, the other dipping down to become a long, low hollow.

He pushed into the hollow, saw it was wide enough to hold the herd, and found a creek coursing along one side of the bottom. He continued on to the end of the hollow where it rose again to rejoin the rest of the plain. A stand of bigtooth aspen beckoned, and he bedded down to sleep. He had come to one decision. He wanted to look in on Abby. He wanted to examine the site of the attack. If he could pick up anything, it would be there. Closing his eyes, he let sleep come until he woke with the first touch of sun on the drooping catkins over his head. He washed and rode back to meet the herd already on its way, threading his way to where Jack Bansen rode. "You'll come to where the land splits. Take the hollow. There's a creek along the bottom where you can water the herd," he said. Bansen nodded, and Fargo rode to the wagon with Burt driving, Ben and Lila beside him.

"I'm going to see Abby Hall. Maybe I can pick up something," he said. "She did me a favor once."

"I'm paying you to break trail. I want you here," Burt Davis said.

"I told Bansen what to do. You're all set for the day," Fargo said.

"When do you figure to be back?" Davis asked.

"Tonight. Maybe sooner," Fargo said and saw the displeasure in Lila's face.

"See to that," she snapped as Davis sent the wagon forward. Fargo rode away, held a steady pace, and went through Highbridge, found his way to the cabin beside the lake, and then found the Hall farm as the late afternoon sun dipped toward the horizon. Two surreys and a buckboard stood outside the house, and Abby came outside as he dismounted. The pain in her eyes was still there and with it a new sense of horror. Six men came from the house behind her, their faces masks of stolid anger.

"He's from the land office," one said. "What's he doin' here?"

"Came to see Abby," Fargo answered.

"Tell him what's happened, and tell him what we're thinking," another of the men said as they walked to the wagons, climbed in, and drove away.

"It's happened again," Abby said to Fargo. "Ed Snavely was killed last night."

"Snavely?" Fargo frowned.

"He was secretary of the Deer Valley claims club," Abby said.

"And he had lock boxes with all the winning bids in them," Fargo offered.

"That's right," she said and nodded grimly. "They took them, killed his family while doing it."

"God, that's terrible," Fargo breathed.

"Everyone's saying one thing, the land auctions are to blame," Abby said. "No more. They have to stop, they're saying."

"That won't catch who's behind this. They're not thinking right," Fargo said.

"They say it'll be a start. I told them you were going to speak to the new land agent. Did you?" Abby questioned.

"Not yet," Fargo said and saw her mouth tighten.

"You don't really want to help us, do you?" she accused.

"I do. That's why I'm here. I don't want to see you going off in the wrong direction," he said.

She gave a little shrug, disappointment and resignation combined in the gesture. "They won't sit back waiting. They won't stand for any more," she said. Fargo's lips pulled back in a grimace. Emotions had killed logic. Anger and guilt had destroyed reason. But wasn't that always the way of things, he reflected.

"Show me where they took the lock boxes," he said. "Maybe I can pick up something." She turned, and he followed to a small shed where the broken door hung open on one hinge.

"It's too late for Pa and the others. Do something about the auctions," Abby said.

"It'll mean a lot more if I can pick up a good lead," he said.

"Do whatever you want," Abby said, dismissal in her voice as she strode away. Fargo knelt at the shed doorway, his eyes sweeping the ground just outside it as well as footprints all but dried out inside the shed. He rose after a moment, his lips tight. Too many new footprints had destroyed anything that might have been helpful. He moved across the yard and found the hoofprints of six horses moving off together. Swinging onto the Ovaro, he followed the prints as they left the yard at a gallop, hooves dug deeply into the ground.

They had ridden across a roadway, turned into a long rise, and then into a thin woods of golden aspen. They had separated there, going off in six different directions. Following two of the trails, he found where they crossed back onto each other and obliterated marks. Cursing, he tracked another trail to a stream where it ended. Others, he found, had ridden over a burnt-out section of charred twigs so broken and dried they left no prints. Dusk began to lower, and he gave up the hunt. They had done an effective job of covering tracks, and he made his way back to Abby's place as night fell. The house was dark as he passed, not a flicker of light within, the silent blackness its own message. He rode on through the new night, feeling saddened more than angry. But it wasn't the pain in Abby's eyes that stayed with him as he rode. It was her words that continued to whirl inside him, that and the faces of stolid, implacable anger.

He had almost caught up to where the herd was stopped for the night, his nostrils flaring as they pulled in the warm scent of the cattle, when he suddenly reined to a halt. Nagging fears had exploded inside him, apprehension crystallizing into alarm. Yanking the horse around, he set off in a gallop and cursed the lack of shortcuts to the land office cabin. He never enjoyed feeling the fool, yet he found himself wishing for the role, hoping that his sudden fears were an unwarranted excursion. He rode, grateful for the Ovaro's power and stamina that took him over hills and into valleys with hardly a change in pace. When he reached the last of the low hills, he saw the cabin and the lamplight from inside it, and allowed himself a deep sigh of relief.

His feet hit the ground before the Ovaro came to a complete halt. "Ivy," he called, the cabin door hanging open. He strode inside, saw the curtain that made two rooms of the cabin was pulled back, and he called out again. There was no answer, and he felt the relief that had enveloped him suddenly vanish. Two long-legged steps took him into the second half of the cabin, and he saw it was empty. Ivy may have decided to leave, he reminded himself, only to curse as he saw her clothes neatly hung on wall pegs. He spun, grabbed up the lamp as he strode from the cabin, and held it aloft as he scanned the ground. The hoofprints took form, at least five horses, maybe six, he saw. Swearing silently, he held onto the lamp as he climbed into the saddle, using it to light the way as he followed the tracks where the riders had ridden from the cabin.

Keeping hold of the lamp, he followed the tracks as the horses spread out. Six, he counted, Ivy on one of them, he was certain. The tracks led into a thick stand of mountain maple, and he followed carefully and leaned to one side as he held the lamp close to the ground. He paused often to listen before going on. He wanted to be sure he stayed far enough back so they wouldn't see the lamplight. When the mountain maples thinned out and a series of gently rolling hills took shape, he turned off the lamp and let the moonlight show the tracks, unwilling to risk the light in the open country. He slowed at the bottom of a hill where the land flattened out. A broken frame of an old wagon lay half on its side, and he edged the pinto forward, and came upon the rotted bottom half of a silo, then the remains of a fence.

An abandoned farm, he thought grunting, and suddenly seeing a flicker of light, let the pinto increase its pace. The house rose up, a dark bulk, but with light coming from inside, and he moved closer, to the edge of the front yard before he dismounted. He took the big Henry from its saddle case, holding the rifle in one hand as he moved closer on foot. His eyes swept the front of the house, and, satisfied there were no sentries, he went forward. He glimpsed two figures inside the house as they crossed near a tall window, and, silent as a puma on the prowl, Fargo moved still closer. The door was half open, and he saw another figure against the far wall. Shifting direction, he sank down behind a half circle of stones where a well had once stood. It allowed him a clear view inside the house, and he saw Ivy seated against the far wall.

The men were all in the room with her. One, tall and thin with graying hair and a harsh mouth, stood closest to her. "Make her talk. She knows," one of the others said, a short figure with a flat-brimmed hat that perched atop his head.

"I don't know anything," Ivy said.

"She's lying," someone else put in.

"I say get rid of her. They'll pay attention to that," another man said, a man younger than the others, with close-cropped hair.

"That's right. Make an example of her. Send them a message," another man added. "I agree with Harry. Get rid of her."

Fargo's eyes went to Ivy. She was afraid, but the hair was still atop her head, and she faced the men with a contained, defiant fear. "You're all wrong. I had sympathy for you. *Now* it's contempt," she said.

"She's got a big mouth. We'll shut her up for good," the one with the flat-brimmed hat said.

Fargo's lips pulled back. The men were on the thin edge of frayed and frustrated tempers. Anything could set them off, their own fury, an attack of panic, Ivy's icy defiance. He didn't dare wait for the explosion that would make Ivy the first casualty, and he scanned the interior of the house again. He could pick off two or three before they knew what hit them. But he didn't want that. There'd been enough killing. Yet he wondered if he had a choice. If he took out three, that still left two to seize Ivy and make her a shield and a hostage. He cursed inwardly. If he could buy thirty seconds, it might be enough, and there was only one way to do that. Not shooting. That'd bring an instant reaction. He'd throw the decision at them, make them think about being the first to die.

No one willingly took that step without thinking about it, at least thirty seconds worth of thinking. He'd rely on human nature as an ally. He rose, then moved on silent steps to the open doorway. Drawing a deep breath, he gathered himself and stepped into the doorway, and saw every head in the room spin to stare at him. Their eyes all took in the big Henry thrust forward, ready to fire. "The first one to make the wrong move is dead," Fargo said with steely quietness. "Very dead. Same with the second one. Any of you gents want to volunteer to be first?" There was silence, and he did not look at Ivy as he spoke to her. "Outside, honey, right now." His eyes, cold as blue ice, swept the room as Ivy leaped up and ran for the door. "Get your horse," he muttered to her as she ran past him.

He had counted off the seconds and reached twenty-three; no one had moved. Human nature had come through for him, he grunted with bitter satisfaction, each of them itching to act, yet none willing to commit the supreme sacrifice. Ivy had had time to reach her horse, and he raised the rifle a fraction. "Nobody moves, nobody gets hurt," he flung at them as he backed from the doorway and kept going backward outside. Of course, they wouldn't stay. They'd come charging. That was human nature, also. He needed to give them an object lesson. Halting, he fired off a volley of shots at the doorway, splinters of wood flying from the door frame, the lintel starting to fall, and the door itself topple. He'd bought another thirty seconds and he turned, raced away, powerful legs driving.

Ivy was on her horse as he leaped onto the Ovaro and was into a gallop in seconds. They'd come after them, he knew, and he sent the Ovaro up a low hill. He was opening the distance at once, but he swore as he slowed, aware that Ivy's horse couldn't keep up with the Ovaro. He heard shouts and hoofbeats from behind. They were coming, and the moon lighted a narrow path that cut to the right. He led the way through it, reached the end, and slowed to listen, grimacing as he heard the horses coming after him. They had seen the path and were certain he'd taken it. They were experienced in fleeing. He wouldn't be outrunning them, not with the lack of speed in Ivy's mount. There'd be no turning aside killing after all. He made a sharp turn into a stand of shadbush, pushing through the thick, shrubby underbrush before coming to a halt. He gestured to Ivy, and she swung from her horse and lowered herself into the heavy underbrush as he reloaded the rifle.

Dropping down alongside a twisted tree trunk, he rested the rifle on a knob of the smooth, gray-brown bark. Their pursuers came into sight—dim, dark shapes at the edge of the shadbush. He hoped they'd pass on, but once again they were too experienced to be easily tricked. They halted, spread out, listened, and he saw them drop from their horses. They had failed to hear the hoofbeats of racing horses and knew what had happened. Eyes narrowed, he saw the dark, darting shapes spread out farther, still too shadowy to afford a clear shot. Ivy was keeping down, he saw, and returned his eyes to the dark forms moving through the trees toward them. He glimpsed one almost directly in front of him, then another off to the right. He half closed his eyes to concentrate on listening and heard two more to his left. That meant there was one more, quieter than the others as he crept through the shadbush.

Fargo's eyes scanned the foliage again, but the only

two shapes in sight were the men in front of him and the one to his right. Inching his way sideways without rustling a blade of grass, he reached Ivy and leaned his face against hers. "You flatten out on the ground when the shooting starts," he whispered. "I'll draw them away from you. When they come after me, get to your horse and run for it."

"What about you?" she whispered back.

"Don't think about me," he said.

"I can't do that," she said. "I wouldn't be able to live with myself."

"You won't live with yourself if you're dead, either. When they come after me, you run, dammit," he hissed and felt her nod. He moved from her, once again inching his way silent as a diamondback on a rock. The figure almost directly in front of him was closer. Raising the rifle, Fargo peered into the trees and found the second figure on the right. He raised the rifle and brought the sights back to the figure creeping toward him. They'd all pinpoint the direction of his shot, he realized, and, gathering the muscles of his legs and thighs, he stood up and fired, all in one motion. The figure in front of him flew backward as if hit by a two-by-four as the heavy rifle shell slammed into him. He had just hit the ground as Fargo flung himself to the left in a twisting dive, landed in the brush, rolled, came up on his stomach a dozen feet away.

He saw the fusillade of shots thud into the ground and the tree trunk where he had been crouched. The figure on the right was rushing forward as he fired. Fargo pulled the rifle trigger, and the man uttered a guttural cry as he went down with arms and legs flailing in the air. Fargo flung himself sideways again, this time rolling through the brush as he heard the bullets thud into the ground where he'd been. He glimpsed two figures at his left, crouched, firing, neither a clear target. He rose and darted behind the trees, swerving and twisting, making no effort at silence as he crashed through brush and snapped off small branches. Another flurry of shots followed him, all wide of the mark as he kept running. The explosion of shots kept him from hearing Ivy racing away on her horse, and as a bullet cracked a branch inches from his head, he dived face forward, hit the ground, tumbled, and came up on one knee.

The two figures were running toward him, still shooting in clusters, plainly banking on luck rather than accuracy, both in plain sight. Fargo fired and one figure spun in a backward, turning motion as he went down. The other figure half skidded to a halt and tried to take aim as Fargo's second shot caught him full in the chest. He went down, and as he did, his finger tightened on the trigger in a last, convulsive reaction. Two more shots whistled through the air, but Fargo was already flattened down behind a tree. He stayed, not moving, very aware that there was still one more man out there, the one who had gone off by himself. Fargo lay still and let breath barely seep through his lips as he waited, ears tuned for the slightest sound.

It seemed an interminable wait, yet he knew that hardly a minute had passed when a voice broke the silence. "I've got her. I've got the girl," it shouted. Fargo recognized the voice as belonging to the one with the flat-brimmed hat. "I've got her," the man shouted again. Fargo remained motionless, the man's shout whirling through him. Was it true? Or was it a clever lie? He stayed completely still, and after another long moment the man shouted again. "Say something," he ordered, but received no answer. "I'll break your goddamn arm," the man snarled, and this time Ivy's sharp cry of pain followed. Fargo swore silently. It had been no clever lie. He had Ivy. The man's voice came again. "You hear me out there?" he asked, waited, then called out again. "Come out or I'll kill her."

Fargo fought down the impulse to obey. Coming out wouldn't save Ivy. The man would kill them both. That was his objective. But he had a problem, Fargo realized. The man expected he was alive, but he wasn't sure of it, and he had to be sure. That uncertainty was suddenly his best weapon, Fargo decided. The man had to be made to find out if he or Ivy were to stay alive. "One more chance or I kill her," the man shouted, breaking into his thoughts. Fargo stayed silent as he desperately hoped he was playing the right cards. But then he hadn't any other cards to play, he realized.

"Come out. Last goddamn chance," the man called, and it was Ivy's despairing answer that unexpectedly helped.

"He's dead. They're all dead. Can't you see that?" she said, her voice breaking.

"Shut up," the man said and fell silent. Fargo could almost hear him listening, straining his ears. Finally, he spoke again. "Walk. In front of me," he ordered, and Fargo heard him start to push Ivy forward through the brush. Fargo didn't move as he lay facedown beside the tree, the rifle at the tips of his fingers. But the rifle would take too long to bring up in close quarters, and his hand moved silently to his holster, slowly drawing the Colt out as the footsteps drew closer. He brought his arm up, positioned it half under his chest so that his body hid his hand with the Colt in it. Again, he let breath barely seep through his lips. The footsteps were near, the man still pushing Ivy in front of him, holding her there as a shield as he scanned the ground in the pale light of the waning moon. Suddenly, he halted, less than a foot away, Fargo estimated. He felt the man's eyes staring at his body as it lay facedown. "Get down," he hissed and pushed Ivy to the ground.

He heard the man step over her and halt beside his one outstretched arm. Fargo held his breath so not even the faintest sound escaped him. He felt the tip of the man's boot push under his shoulder, lift, start to turn him over, and he let his body stay limp. The man pushed harder, and Fargo felt his body turning over. He had reached his side when his finger tightened on the trigger. Through eyes that were narrowed slits, he saw the man, a dark shape looming over him. The Colt erupted as the man leaned forward, and Fargo felt the heat of the blast against his own chest. The man catapulted backward, hitting against Ivy, who let out a half scream as she rolled away. Fargo pushed onto one knee, ready to fire again.

But there was no need. The man lay on his back, the gun falling from his fingers, a slow stain moving across his midsection. He was still breathing, and Fargo rose, stepping to his side. "Stupid, all of you, just stupid."

"Go to hell," the man breathed.

"What club?" Fargo asked.

"Deer Valley," the man gasped out, shuddered, and his last breath escaped from twisted lips. Fargo turned away, and Ivy was in his arms, trembling against him.

"I'd reached my horse," she said. "I was half into the saddle when he grabbed me."

"He must've been nearby," Fargo said. "Let's get away from here."

She nodded, clinging to him as he led the way to the horses, and he helped her into the saddle. "My things are all at the cabin," she said. "But I don't want to stay there."

"You can pick up your things, and we'll go find somewhere else," he said.

"Someplace where I can think, and feel safe. Someplace with you," Ivy said, then fell silent as he rode back to the office cabin with her. She gathered her things, stuffing a saddlebag full as the moon slipped over the horizon. When she was ready, he led the way through the dark before the dawn, finding a spot he had visited once before. As dawn touched the sky, he drew to a halt in a wooded glen almost entirely closed in by an arch of black ash. Unsaddling the horses, he set out his bedroll and waited for Ivy to put out her blanket as he started to take off his shirt. But she didn't take the blanket from her saddlebag. Instead, she sat down beside him, unsmiling, a tiny furrow creasing her smooth forehead. "I'm still shaking," she said.

"That figures. Stretch out. Relax," he said. Her eyes stayed on him. "You still have things to sort out?" he asked.

"Some," she said. "But less than before."

As he watched, she reached up, and pulled a clip from the top of her head, and he stared as the long brown hair cascaded in a swirl to frame her face. It was a different face, suddenly soft, warm, all the contained distance gone from it. He was still staring at the transformed beauty of her when he felt the soft touch of her lips on his.

7

A sweet throbbing. He felt it course through him. Her lips stayed, pressed, moved on his, and her hand came to touch the bare skin of his chest, gently down across the muscled pectoral contours. "Oh, oh migod," she breathed, and he felt her other hand undoing buttons, the blouse coming open and falling from her shoulders. He moved forward, and she lay on the bedroll. He drank in softly rounded shoulders, breasts that were very round and full at the undersides, pink nipples with areolas that matched perfectly, tips hardly raised above the faintly textured circles. Below her lovely breasts he saw a deep rib cage, and, as he undid the clasp of her skirt, it slid down to reveal a short waist, a convex little belly, and below it, a flocculent, black little triangle. Her legs moved, the skirt falling away entirely, and he saw smooth thighs, round knees, and shapely calves. But mostly, he was struck by the velvety roundness of her, every part of her blending into every other part with a seamless, unbroken roundness, nothing sharp, nothing angled to her, ribs, hips, even elbows, all rounded.

"Very lovely," he breathed as he undid his trousers to lay naked beside her. He saw her eyes flick down for a moment, her lips part as her breath drew in sharply.

"Oh, migod," she murmured, and at his touch, his hand gently cupping one breast, she uttered a shuddered cry that was half alarm and half pleasure. He let his thumb come up to pass slowly across one pink nipple, then circle its lovely roundness, and pleasure drowned the alarm in her cry. Slowly, he brought his hands to her breasts, caressing, pressing, circling the pink areolas, and Ivy uttered tiny little gasps. When his hands moved to press the pink tips, the tiny gasps became half screams. "Oh, migod, oh migod, oh, oh . . . oooooh, yes, oh yes," she murmured, and he saw her mouth open, her lips working, seeking. He pressed his mouth to hers and felt her tongue waiting to respond as she gave urgent little cries. Her arms flew around him when he brought his mouth to one round breast, took in the little tip, and caressed it with his tongue, feeling its magical rise.

Ivy's arms stayed locked around him as he gently pulled on her breast, sucked first one then the other into his mouth, and realized she was breathing out sharp cries filled with rapturous urgency. His hand moved down, a slow, fervid trail across her abdomen, paused at the oblong indentation, moved slowly across the roundness that was her belly, and he saw her legs move up and down, pressing against each other. His lips continued to suck on the pink nipples as his hand found the small flocculent mound, surprisingly soft, almost woolly, and he let his hand move through it. "Oh, Jeeeez, oh, oh migod," Ivy cried out, and his hand moved down farther, to the very tip of the little triangle, and felt the wetness touch his fingers. Ivy screamed as he pressed deeper, and suddenly her hips were twisting to the right, then the left.

"No, no," she gasped. "Yes, yes . . . oh, migod, yes," and her pelvis half rose, then fell back again. He explored further, touched the tip of the dark portal and felt the moistness of her thighs where they touched his hand. He touched succulent walls of wetness, and Ivy's screams were a constant series of urgent pleadings. He moved deeper, caressing, and her torso rose and fell, and he felt her hands clutching at his shoulders and back. He probed further, and a long, wailing sound came from her, and she was suddenly bucking and twisting her entire torso, rising and falling, finding a rhythm of its own, and he matched her every motion until with starting suddenness, she screamed, a long, sharp cry, and he felt her body stiffen even as it quivered. He knew surprise as she held in midair, her contractions of ecstasy unmistakable until, with a terrible sigh, she fell back on the bedroll and her hand came down to press against his, holding him to her.

"You were quick, too quick," he murmured.

"Yes, too quick," she breathed.

"We can do better," he said gently.

"Yes, please, oh yes," Ivy half whispered. "It all just happened. I couldn't stop. It all just ran away from me."

"Happens that way sometimes. With some women," he said. "They come quickly, sort of an undress rehearsal." He moved inside her, and Ivy moaned, then half turned to him.

"Oh, God, yes," she said, and he felt the warm, moist wanting of her instantly answer his touch. "Aaaaah, aaaaaah," she breathed as he caressed, and when he drew back, she stiffened, but he brought his body over hers, pressed his warm, pulsating, soft firmness against her little woolly mound. "Aaaaiiii . . . oh, Jeeeeeez," Ivy screamed. He brought himself downward, touched her own throbbing inner lips, and her thighs fell open, then came together against his legs, excitingly wet. He slid forward, and Ivy's mouth parted for the parade of gasps that came from her. She pulled his head down between her breasts, held it there as she began to move under him, her every move accompanied by a tiny half scream that grew in strength with his every thrust. The rhythm that she had found the first time returned, and he brought his own body to hers, joining all the senses together in the wonderful, wild dance of ecstasy.

This time, when she reached that final pinnacle of fulfillment, he was with her, part of her explosion and her cries. She gave a long, rising shriek that culminated in a succession of wails, each one rising from the one before. She quivered against him, fingers digging into his shoulders, the round breasts pushing hard into his face, every inch of her round body consumed with pleasure. She held on to ecstasy, her orgasm longer than any he'd ever witnessed, as she clung to him, pressed close as a wet leaf against a rock. Finally, her body grew limp, her quivering subsided, and a low half moan, half sigh came from her lips as he lifted his head from her breasts to stare down at her. He pushed a strand of hair from her face, and he saw something close to awe in the brown depths of her eyes. "When you let your hair down, you really mean it," he said.

A little smile crossed her face, almost sheepish. "Never let it down before, not like this," she said. He moved, and she clutched at him, hands digging into

his back. "Stay . . . stay," she murmured. "Forever."
He chuckled and stayed with her, enjoying the warm,
liquescent glove that held him until finally he slipped
from her. He enjoyed drinking in her rounded softness, that seamlessness of her where every line
blended into another. When she closed her eyes, he
slept with her, the arch of leaves so dense that only
small shafts of sunlight filtered through. He woke
when she did and saw that the sun had passed the
noon hour as he peered between branches. She sat up,
round-cupped breasts swaying, a sweet unison of
beauty. "I wish we didn't have to leave," she said.

"But we do," he said, not really disagreeing with
her and watched her take her canteen and a cloth from
her saddlebag and washed, her every movement
lovely to behold. He did the same, and when he was
dressed, he saddled the horses and watched her eyes
find his.

"What now?" she asked as he led the way from beneath the arch of black ash.

"Going back. Going to finish breaking trail. There
might still be answers to find. You're going with me.
You can't stay on with the claims clubs on a ram-
page," Fargo said.

"I don't understand any of it now," Ivy said.

"Can't say that I do," Fargo muttered.

"I understand what they did to protect their lands,
wrong as it was, but stealing the bids doesn't make
any sense. They were going to be called invalid, anyway," Ivy said.

"Unless somebody doesn't know that," Fargo said.

"But who?"

"Dammed if I know. It puts a hole in things I was
wondering about," Fargo said. "Let's ride. We've a lot

of ground to cover." He put the pinto into a trot and rode in silence with Ivy, crossed hills on the way north, held to a good steady pace that made time, and he smelled the cattle before he saw them. Crossing a low rise, the herd appeared before him, the four wagons alongside. Burt Davis brought his wagon to a halt as he rode up with Ivy. Ben sat beside him, and Lila came from the other side of the wagon, her face tight.

"Where the hell have you been?" Burt Davis snapped.

"There were more attacks, more killings," Fargo said. "They hit back, picked on Ivy to do it."

"They blame the auctions for everything that's happened," Ivy said.

"Screw them," Ben Brewster said.

"That's her problem, not yours," Davis said.

"I made it mine. She's riding with me until I can get her to a stage," Fargo said.

"You're not staying on, my dear?" Ben asked Ivy, concern in his voice.

"Definitely not. I'm going back to Washington," Ivy said.

"What are you going to tell them?" Ben asked almost casually.

"What's happened. About all the trouble the auctions have caused," Ivy said. "And how you just up and quit," she added.

Fargo saw Ben Brewster's face set. "There's no need for that. I gave you a great opportunity, girl. You ought to stick with it, stay on here," he said.

"Her life's in danger here," Fargo said.

"A few hotheads, an isolated incident," Ben said, his eyes boring into Ivy. "Don't be scared off. Stay on. You're doing the wrong thing by going back."

"I'll think about it," Ivy said, and Fargo swore silently at how uncomfortable she had become.

"You ride on. I'll catch up in a minute," he told her, and she moved away.

"I'm paying you to break trail, not drag your own little bedwarmer around with you, Fargo," Burt Davis broke in. "She can go back on her own."

"And I can quit," Fargo said.

"No," Ben cut in sharply, then let his voice soften at once. "No need for that. You go on, break trail, find us the good routes and the towns to avoid. I'm sure they'll be more. We need you." Fargo's eyes went to Burt Davis, and saw the man shrug in unhappy agreement. He snapped the reins and the wagon rolled forward, and Fargo saw Lila wait, anger in her eyes.

"What the hell do you think you're doing, bringing her along?" Lila hissed. "I warned you."

"Relax. We'll be getting together," Fargo said placatingly.

"We damn well better," Lila muttered through lips that hardly moved. He tossed her a smile and rode on, passed Burt Davis and Ben on the wagon, and offered a pleasant nod and knew they didn't see the ice in his eyes. When he reached Ivy, she pulled alongside him.

"Not exactly a warm welcome," she remarked.

"Didn't expect one," Fargo said.

"It's plain that Ben thought I'd stay on. He shouldn't have assumed that," Ivy said.

"But he did, and now he sure doesn't want you going back to Washington, not now, anyway," Fargo said.

"Why? What difference does it make to him? He's quit," Ivy said. "Nothing makes sense around here, no reason for all these attacks."

"There's a reason, believe me," Fargo said grimly. "I just don't know what it is." He put the Ovaro into a trot, rode perhaps another half hour when the three horsemen appeared, riding hard toward him. He halted, and watched the blond hair fly in the wind. Her wan face even paler, Abby halted, the two men behind her middle-aged, faces as strained as hers.

"There was another attack last night," Abby said.

"You talking about the shoot-out at the old farm? I know about that," Fargo said coldly.

"No. They struck again, killed four members of the Boulder Hollows claims club and stole all the Boulder auction bids," Abby said.

Fargo's face refused to show sympathy. "Your friends from the Deer Valley club attacked Ivy. Killing brings killing."

"Yes," Abby said, her shoulders drooping. "We quit. We're not going to bid anymore, none of us. It's not worth all this. We can't win, it seems."

Fargo searched her face, then that of the two men with her. There was only bitter resignation in their faces. "Why come to me?" Fargo questioned.

"You get around. You can put out the word. We don't want any more attacks, any more killings," Abby said.

"It's over for us," one of the men said.

"Put out the word, please. No more killings," Abby said, and her eyes were suddenly wet. She quickly turned and rode away, the two men following. Fargo waited till they were out of sight before he prodded the pinto forward.

"Put out the word to whom?" Ivy asked. "They still suspect we've a hand in it."

"Some do, I suppose, but mostly they're desperate. They're casting out," Fargo said.

"They've given up. They've done the wrong things for the right reasons, and now they're doing the right thing for the wrong reasons. It's sad," Ivy said.

"It could get sadder. I've a feeling whoever's behind these attacks won't stop till they have every bid," Fargo said.

"Why? How does it all fit? Or maybe it doesn't," Ivy said.

"Maybe it doesn't," Fargo echoed. "Damned if I know." He halted as an oblong plain rose, bordered on two sides by forests of box elder that would help keep the herd together. "You stay here. I'll bring the herd up," Fargo said and rode back at a fast canter. He met the herd, found Jack Bansen, and led the trail foreman to the oblong plain as the sun dipped below the horizon. Alarm quickly grabbed at him as he didn't see Ivy and then he saw her, a few hundred yards from the end of the plain and at the edge of the box elder.

He waited till the herd settled down, helped Bansen bring in a half dozen wanderers, and then rode past two of the wagons to where Ben sat in front of the Davis rig, Burt and Lila nearby. "Ivy still figure to go back?" Ben asked, squinting up at him.

"Haven't heard her say different," Fargo answered.

"You still going to help her?"

"Figure to," Fargo said.

"Hold off till the end of the drive. I want her to have more time to think about it. That's not too much to ask," Ben said.

"Depends on how much further Davis expects to drive this herd to nowhere," Fargo said.

"He'll find a buyer. Burt's the kind that always gets lucky."

"I heard he makes his own luck," Fargo said.

"Either way." Ben shrugged.

"I'll talk to Ivy," Fargo said and rode on. He saw Lila rise, watch him go, hands on her hips, and he could feel her simmering anger. But he didn't glance back, then paused at the chuck wagon as the cook held out a big tin of bacon and beans right from the fire.

"For you and the lady," the cook said.

"Obliged. Thanks for both of us," Fargo said and took the pan back to where Ivy had set her blanket down back into the trees. "Eat while it's still hot," he told her. "Enjoy. It's going to be your main pleasure for the night."

Ivy frowned at him. "You think we're going to be bothered?" she questioned.

"Don't know, but I don't aim to be watched, and I don't aim to be surprised," he said, and she attacked her beans, disappointment in her face. When they finished the meal, he collected an armful of dry twigs that he put in a circle around the blanket and the bedroll. Footsteps would snap any of them instantly and he'd be awake.

"You really expect trouble?" Ivy asked.

"No, but then I like being cautious," he said, not saying that it was Lila he was chiefly concerned with. He'd tasted her ruthlessness. He wasn't about to taste it again. He stretched out and put the Colt at his side, saw Ivy watching him, disappointment still in her eyes. "Another time, another place," he said.

"You can be sure of that," she said, lying down. She let her hand find his as she dropped off to sleep. He slept soon after as the night stayed still, and he woke with the new sun. If Lila had come checking, she'd not come close enough to step on the twigs, he grunted as he dressed. Ivy woke, pulled on clothes, and she rode beside him as he paused at the herd. The cattle were restless, he noted, their long, hooked horns knocking into each other with more reckless unease. Ivy rode beside him as he waved Bansen on and sent the Ovaro out of the oblong plains and onto land that was uneven and veined with small furrows.

Deer tracks showed all over the terrain, and he followed them to a large lake, shallow but clear, and he let the Ovaro drink, then waited until the herd came into view. He rode on again as the cattle eagerly crowded around the water to drink, saw a forest of black oak rise up to narrow the open land to a long ribbon. The herd could thread its way, he decided, and rode on. When the land widened again, it divided into three sections. He explored each, chose the one with the fewest rocks, and waved the others on when they finally caught up to him.

The sun had gone down behind low hills as he rode on, and he came alongside Ivy when he found a wide swath between stands of low-branched bitternut where the cattle could gather for the night. "You've been mighty quiet all day," he remarked.

"Been thinking about the homesteaders. You were right, chickens coming home to roost. They started the beatings and killings, and now they're paying for it. I shouldn't feel at all sorry for them, especially after they were going to kill me."

"But you do."

"Yes. I still think Ben should have told them."

"Told them what?"

"About the Preemption Act," she said.

"The Preemption Act? What's that?" Fargo asked.

"After the Land Auction Act was passed, Congress recognized the unfairness of parts of it, how it lent itself to real injustices. They passed the Preemption Act to the Land Auction law. It gave a squatter or homesteader the right to buy his land in advance of auction, for a dollar twenty-five cents an acre, if he could show that he'd lived on it, worked it, and improved it."

"You told Ben Brewster about this?" Fargo frowned.

"Yes."

"What'd he say?"

"He said it'd only complicate holding the auctions. Maybe we'd look into it some time later," Ivy answered.

Fargo felt the frown digging deeper into his forehead. Ivy waited, plainly unaware of the real meaning of what she had said. But suddenly everything was exploding inside him, answers, explanations, all the little gnawing questions coming together, each one taking its place. "That's it," he breathed. "Jesus, that's it."

"What are you talking about?" Ivy frowned back.

"What you told me, it makes it all fit, from the very beginning," Fargo said.

"I don't understand," she said.

He took her aside, and leaned her against one of the wide-trunked bitternut. "I'll start with the question that's bothered me from square one, why Ben Brewster took the job as land office agent. I could never swallow the story about a chance to turn over a new leaf and become an honest citizen. Now I know the real reason. Now I know what he saw in it." Ivy waited, still frowning. "He saw a way to buy up all the best land and become a huge landowner. He hired men, supplied them with money, to go out to the auctions and outbid anyone else. As land office agent, he controlled where and when the auctions would be held. It was simple for him to have his hired hands there to make their high bids."

"And later he'd take back all the land he'd bought through his bidders," Ivy said, awe replacing the frown in her face.

"That's why he wasn't about to say anything about the Preemption Act. It would have ruined his scheme."

"But the claims clubs wrecked his scheme," Ivy said. "They beat and killed anyone coming to bid and rigged the auctions for themselves."

"He didn't expect that. In fact, he didn't know exactly what was going on, but he had to find out. That's when he sent for me," Fargo explained. "He up and quit when he realized the claims clubs had completely wrecked his plans."

"But Washington would declare the bids invalid because the auctions weren't open," Ivy said.

"Yes, and they'd insist the Preemption Act be invoked. His scheme was done for either way. He was at a dead end. That's why he quit," Fargo said.

"That explains Ben Brewster. It doesn't explain the attacks on the claims clubs, or why he joined up with Burt Davis."

"You know what they say about how great minds think alike. The same goes for evil minds. One crook can smell another. He joined with Burt Davis because they both had the same goal, and he saw a last chance to win."

"He and Davis were in it together?" Ivy asked in surprise.

"Not at first. I never understood why Burt Davis was so anxious to have me break trail for him where there was no place to sell a herd. He made a big deal about having people know I was working for him. I understand now. I've a reputation. I made his cattle drive seem legitimate. I'm part of the window dressing."

"It's not legitimate? It's not a real cattle drive?"

"No. It never was. It's a front, a cover."

"For what?"

"For hiding the stolen bids. You need somewhere to hide lock boxes, within quick riding distance from the attacks. What better place than a wagon with an innocent cattle drive?" Fargo asked.

Shock wreathed her face. "He's behind the attacks?"

"That's right," Fargo said. "Burt Davis has a grapevine. I'll bet my bottom dollar he knew the claims clubs existed. He was planning the attacks on his own. When he met up with Ben, they went into business together. They saw how they could help each other. Davis had the men to carry out the attacks and steal the bids. They figured they could change the names on the forms. Ben had the authority to make that easy. He could just approve each bid."

"But he quit," Ivy said.

"Washington doesn't know that," Fargo said.

"But I do," Ivy breathed. "That's why he doesn't want me to go back."

"Not till they've finished. You won't be going back then, either," Fargo said grimly.

Ivy's mouth fell open and she stared at him, her

face draining of color. "You mean . . . ?" she half whispered.

"They can't let you go back." He nodded. "They'll arrange an accident."

"My God," she gasped. "And you?"

"Same thing, only they probably won't bother with arranging an accident," Fargo said. She peered at him, wanting not to believe, unwilling to grasp the dimensions of what he'd laid out for her.

"But you don't really know any of this. I mean, you're supposing. What if you're wrong?" she asked.

"What if I'm not?" he tossed back. "You want to take that chance?" She swallowed hard as she stared. "There's only one way to be sure," he said.

"What's that?"

"Find the lock boxes with the stolen bids. If I'm right, they're in one of the wagons," Fargo said.

"It'll be guarded," Ivy said.

"No," he said, and her glance questioned. "They won't do that. That'd call attention to it. But I'm betting they'll be off on another attack tonight, leaving just a few hands with the herd. I'll check the wagons."

"It could be any of them?" she questioned. "Even the chuck wagon?"

"Could be, but that's at the bottom of the list."

"Burt Davis's wagon?" she offered.

"That's second from the bottom. They're being real careful. If some town sheriff did come searching, chances are he'd pick the boss's wagon. I'd guess they'd choose one of the other two wagons. I'll have time to search both of them, I hope."

"Should I go with you?" Ivy asked.

"No. It'll be tricky enough alone. The men they

134

leave will be watching. You stay here, get some sleep," he said.

"Fat chance of that," she muttered.

He paused, and peered at her. "Tell me, why didn't you say anything about the Preemption Act long ago?" he questioned.

"Didn't think it would be all that important, certainly not like this," she said, paused.

"Go on," he pressed.

"I didn't think it was my place to say anything," she answered.

"You were so concerned with being proper," he grunted.

"I was raised that way," she said.

"Glad you stopped, for more than one reason."

"Yes, being proper has its drawbacks, I've found out," she said, leaning her head against his chest. "Be careful tonight. I want another chance at being improper."

"That'll help me be careful," he said, then stepped back as he saw the herd of longhorns come into sight. He left her, rode out to meet Jack Bansen, and guided the cattle into the swath between the bitternut. He stayed, idled back and forth until he noted where each of the wagons had halted for the night. He had moved near Burt's wagon when Lila came toward him.

"I'm tired waiting. You find a time and place," she said. "Try weaseling out and you'll be sorry. Believe me."

"Wouldn't think of it." He smiled and drew only a glare from her. "You know, I don't think you really want me that much. I just think you want to have your way," he said.

Her eyes narrowed. "I want you. Why is my busi-

135

ness. You just do your part, and soon." She turned and strode away and Fargo rode on, uneasiness swirling through him. Lila complicated things. She was a loose cannon. She was following her own agenda, but that could switch to Burt's agenda at any time. He wouldn't know if that happened, of course. Keeping Lila happy could be a duty, but it could also be a trap. Yet not accommodating her would be a danger, that was certain. None of the choices appealed, he swore silently as he returned to Ivy.

He put down his bedroll beside her, stretched out, and she lay close to him. "Want some jerky?" he asked.

"My stomach's too tight to eat," she said.

"Lie still and take deep breaths. I know that waiting can be harder than acting, but you've no choice. We've no choice," he corrected. She fell silent, and he heard her breathing grow regular. He stayed with her, half dozing, and let the moon reach the midnight sky before he rose.

He had to pull his hand from hers, and he stepped from the trees, immediately going into a long, loping crouch as he moved into the open. Ivy's question stayed with him: *What if you're wrong?* He was almost certain he wasn't wrong, but almost wasn't good enough. He had to be sure, and as he neared the herd, he dropped to one knee. Slowly, he scanned the far edge of the mass of cattle, moonlight glinting on the long, curved horns. His eyes swept the edges of the herd again, then once more, and he felt the grim satisfaction spiral through him. He had been right about one thing.

8

Only three cowhands rode the edges of the herd, no other horses tethered past the cattle. At least six horses and their riders were missing. Night followed day, as inevitably as cause and effect. Another attack was taking place. But that was still not enough. He couldn't turn away. Knowing was not proof. The final truth couldn't be left hanging. He had to find it for himself, beyond the last, clinging doubt. It could not be left unresolved. His eyes moved across the dark mass of the cattle again. But Davis's wagon, largest of the three high-topped Kansas freight wagons, rested at the far end of the herd. The other two were directly across from him, but some three hundred longhorns were in between, he noted unhappily.

He had wanted to make his way around the edges of the cattle to the wagons, but the three riders were positioned to scan the entire perimeter of the herd. One or another would surely spot him. With a silent curse, he stepped forward, into the mass of cattle. Sliding his feet along the ground rather than taking steps, he began to squeeze his way into the herd. He felt the latent power of their warm bodies as they rubbed against him, and their warm, musky odor, that special odor of cattle, assailed his nostrils. Moving ever so slowly, ever so carefully, he watched, waited for a moment's opening, slid his way through and waited for another opening. Even so, the steers were aware of his presence. He felt them move restlessly, horns clicking as they hit against each other. One of the cowhands picked up the restlessness, moved closer, and Fargo stayed motionless between two big longhorns.

He lowered his eyes slightly, just enough to set the top of his head behind massive shoulder blades. He didn't dare drop to one knee. If one of the steers moved suddenly and knocked him over, he was done for. The others nearby would react instantly, surge forward, backward, sideways. Sharp hooves would trample him, driven by thousands of pounds. They were a quick-tempered breed, the longhorns, easily riled and not easily placated. He found himself remembering how Texas cowhands described them as three-quarters horns and hooves and one-quarter hair. The cowhand called to the steers, then slowly backed his horse away, and Fargo drew a deep sigh of relief as he straightened up.

He began to slide forward again, and felt himself knocked sideways as a big steer half turned. But the body of another longhorn at his back kept him from falling though the steer uttered a short bellow. Fargo moved through a space that came open, found another space between the huge bodies, and slid through it. He kept squeezing forward, finding tiny openings as the steers moved until he saw he was halfway through, in the very center of the herd. He felt himself perspiring. It was taking much longer than he thought it would to make his way through the densely packed mass of huge bodies. Every time his presence brought on a surge of restless movement and sudden uneasy bellows, he halted, stayed in place, and waited for the steers to calm down. The huge, curved horns brushed against him time and again, and he had to keep watch and duck away from those that suddenly came at him as a massive head turned or dipped and rose again.

Fighting down impatience and the urge to move forward more quickly, he kept inching his way, all too aware that anything else could trigger sudden death. Finally, as he sensed the other edge of the herd, the density of the mass of musky bodies began to thin out. He saw the dark bulk of the nearest wagon loom up in front of him and allowed himself to draw a deep breath. He cast a quick glance at the three cowhands, saw they were in place, and he squeezed himself between the last of the longhorns at the far edge of the herd and darted to the deep shadows of the big, canvas-topped freight wagon. Crouching, he moved around the wagon to the rear and pulled himself inside through the tailgate opening. He gave thanks for a strong, almost full moon that let enough light in through the tail opening and the loose sides of the canvas top to let him see that the inside of the wagon held a careless jumble of boxes, bags, sheets, bedrolls, travel bags, and other items.

He found a place to sit and began to go through each box and bag, sifting carefully and putting each back in place. It also took longer than he'd expected, and he had just finished going through the last box without finding what he sought when his sharp ears caught the sound of hoofbeats. With a curse, he swung from the rear of the wagon and saw riders approaching. They were coming fast, and he started to climb back into the wagon when he stopped himself. The lock boxes weren't in the wagon, but they might go to it with other things. Dropping back to the ground, he crawled between the wide wheels and flattened himself under the wagon. He found himself able to get a snake's-eye view of the riders as they came to a halt, dismounted, tethered their horses, and pulled off saddles. One man became only feet and legs as he walked to the wagon, reached inside, and pulled out a bedroll. Fargo breathed a sigh of relief that he hadn't stayed inside the wagon.

The man trudged away, and Fargo watched the others, waiting to see lock boxes being carried to the second wagon. But no lock boxes appeared, no one carrying anything as the men began to settle down for the night. Surprise began to dig a furrow in his forehead as he watched. His eyes followed Jack Bansen from under the wagon as the man strode the distance to the Davis wagon. Burt Davis came outside and both men spoke, their voices too low for him to catch words. But he did pick up an occasional oath and the sounds of anger, voices tight with tension. Finally, Bansen hurried away and lay where most of the others had already fallen asleep.

Fargo stretched, one throbbing thought filling his mind. They hadn't brought back any lock boxes, and the question pounded through his thoughts. What did it mean? Where had Bansen and the others gone in the dead of night? Were Burt Davis and Brewster onto something entirely different? Had he read everything wrong? Fargo asked himself. No, he answered angrily.

Too many things fitted. Yet his final piece suddenly didn't fit at all. He swore silently at the sudden turn of things. The second wagon was looming larger and even more important now, and he lay still, waiting till he was sure Bansen and the others were asleep before he crept from under the wagon. The three cowhands riding herd were still very awake and watching, and he stayed in a crouch as he made his way to the second wagon.

Climbing inside, he found it much like the other, crammed with boxes and bags, but also holding a number of mattresses. He began to go through the boxes, first, aware that his light was fast disappearing as the moon moved toward the horizon. When he finished the boxes, he began to look under the mattresses. He was lifting one of two atop each other when he halted and rolled the top mattress back on itself as he stared down at the three metal lock boxes that were hidden between it and the other. A tremendous sense of vindication swept through him, all the sudden doubts shattering. The locks on each box had been broken open, and he lifted the lids. In the last of the moonlight he saw the bids inside each box, each form properly filled out and signed by the auctioneer. At the bottom of each form was the space for the land office agent to put his stamp and signature.

Fargo closed the lids on each box and rolled the mattress back in place as his thoughts raced. Another question had been answered. He understood why Bansen and the others had returned empty-handed and the meaning of the oath-filled conversation with Burt Davis. The attack had taken place, but the claims club had been foresighted. They had taken the lock boxes away, and the attackers had no prize to claim. Perhaps they'd even been frustrated in their killing plans. Fargo climbed from the rear of the wagon as the moon dropped below the horizon, plunging night into stygian blackness. He moved from the wagon and followed the edge of the cattle by smell and sound more than sight. When he reached the end of the herd, he crept away, peered through dark shapes, and finally found the stand of bitternut as the first faint streaks of dawn touched the sky.

Ivy had fallen asleep, he saw, and he lay beside her and drew a little over an hour of sound sleep to himself before the sun woke him. Ivy woke and was in his arms instantly. "God, you're back," she said. "I stayed awake as long as I could."

"I was right about everything," he said.

"You found the lock boxes?" she asked, and he nodded. "What now?" Ivy questioned. "Can you find a town with a sheriff?"

"Have them jailed?" Fargo said. "Not just like that. They'd come up with all kinds of explanations."

"We could call on claims clubs members to testify," Ivy said.

"It'd be hard to accuse Ben Brewster without admitting what they've done, and I don't think they'll want to do that," Fargo said.

"Then they just get away with everything. They can't be stopped." Ivy frowned.

"Not here. You've got to get back to Washington and tell your story. They'll listen to you there," Fargo said.

"Yes, I'm sure they will," Ivy agreed. "Then we run, get away from here."

Fargo's lips pulled back. "They'll come after us, all of them. We won't be able to outrun them."

"You mean, I won't. You could get away alone," she said.

"Maybe, but that's not an option," he said, and her

lips were against his cheek, then his mouth, sweet softness.

"What do we do?" she asked when she pulled away.

"Go on. Play along until I can come up with something," he said. "Finish dressing and meet me by the herd." She nodded, and he climbed onto the pinto and rode out to where Jack Bansen was preparing to move the herd forward. He was nearing Bansen when Lila Davis stepped out from behind a lone bitternut, her face tight, deep breasts straining the fabric of a white blouse she wore over a loose green skirt.

"Where the hell were you last night?" she spit at him, catching him by surprise.

"Out riding," he said, recovering as smoothly as he could. "I told you once before, I like to go exploring at night, less distraction." He saw the skepticism behind the glare which she fixed on him. "You come sneaking around last night?" he tossed at her.

"Why not?" she snapped. "You're lucky I didn't find you screwing that little bitch."

"Why?"

"It would have been your last screw. Hers, too," Lila said, drawing a big Joslyn Army revolver, a five-shot, single-action weapon, a powerful though not terribly accurate gun, from the pocket of her skirt. "I told you what I want comes first. I meant it," she said.

"I know you did. I haven't forgotten," he said mildly.

"I'm tired of waiting," Lila hissed, dropped the pistol back into her skirt pocket, and strode away. Fargo watched her go with his lips tight, not at all sure that she had believed his explanation for being away. She was a woman obsessed, and women obsessed seldom believed anything, even their own obsession. He was certain of one thing, however. She'd tell Burt and Brewster about his absence, and he cursed her spying horniness. Both men were already suspicious and uneasy, already watching for the right place and time to arrange that accident for Ivy and the bullet for him. This could hurry their search. He swore again as he rode to where Jack Bansen waited.

"Keep north. The land's good for another few miles. I'm going to ride ahead and find some water. I'll circle back to you," he said and rode to where Ivy waited at the head of the herd. "Ride," he muttered.

"What happened?" she asked, reading his face.

"We could be running out of time," he said.

She waited until they were out of sight of the herd before she spoke again. "You said we can't outrun them."

"And we can't outfight them. They've too many guns," he said.

"I'll say it again. You could get away alone," she offered.

"I answered that," he said brusquely.

"Are there any other choices, really?" Ivy asked almost gently.

"We need to get ourselves some help," Fargo muttered.

"Maybe you could call in the Sioux," Ivy sniffed.

"Glad to see you still have a sense of humor," he shot back.

"I'm not trying to be funny. I'm trying to tell you to run, to save yourself, at least. There's no help we can get out here," she said.

"That's because you've a narrow idea of help. You think help is man-made, that it only consists of sheriffs and good people who come to your rescue," he said. "But it isn't. Help comes in all kinds of ways. It can be a trail, a hole in the ground, a line of rocks, whatever you can find that works." She stared at him, and he saw her trying to understand. "A jackrabbit running from a hawk can't call on other jackrabbits. He plunges into the high grass. His help is a thousand blades of grass and bulrushes. A grizzly corners a fox. The fox gets help from a hollow log too small for the grizzly to reach into. A fawn sees a wolf. It runs to the herd where the big bucks form a circle around it. A coyote chases a gopher. The gopher finds his help in a trail he knows that goes underground. I could keep going. Help can come in all kinds of ways."

She nodded, and he turned the Ovaro and started up the side of a hill. "I want to take the high land," he said, and she rode beside him as he climbed onto a line of ridges that let him see the terrain below, and his eyes scanned every cut, passage, forest, and dip and rise, every valley and every narrow plateau. He rode in silence, all his concentration on the land below.

More than an hour had passed when Ivy's voice broke the silence. "We looking for high grass, narrow logs, or trails that go underground?" she asked, and he heard the bitterness of despair and resignation in her voice.

"All three, and anything else that spells help," he said quietly as he continued to scan the land. He had reached the end of the high ridge when he halted and peered down at a long canyon. A thin line of black oak bordered the canyon on each side, backed by solid rock that rose up almost as high as the trees. His eyes followed the line of the canyon, saw it narrow at the far end, and end abruptly at a wall of trees with solid rock behind them. His brow knotted as he scanned the canyon again. "We go down there," he said softly. "And I found us that help."

"The canyon?" Ivy said frowning.

"The canyon's only part of it."

"That's a box canyon, a dead end," she said.

"You see it and I see it, but from up here. From down there it looks like an ordinary canyon. They won't know it's a box canyon till they reach the end of it," Fargo said.

"You'll lead them into the canyon, and while they're in it we make a break for it," Ivy said.

"No. They'd come chasing out after us," he said. "I'm going to see that they don't come out. Let's get back."

"I don't understand. Where's that help we need?" she asked as she rode after him.

"Waiting for us," he said. "Let's make time. I'll spell it out later." He put the Ovaro into a fast canter as he rode down from the high hills, and reached the land below to see the herd slowly moving along. Davis drove his wagon alongside the mass of cattle, Brewster sitting beside him. Lila rode with Jack Bansen a dozen feet ahead. The rest of the wagons and Bansen's men were strung out along the length of the herd. "There's a good canyon with a lake at the end of it," Fargo called out as he came to a halt. "But the ground gets real soft when you get near the lake. The wagons will bog down after three hundred longhorns chew up the ground, so take the wagons in first and let the herd follow."

"Good enough," Davis said and immediately snapped the reins on his team and moved the wagon forward beside the cattle. Bansen waved for the other wagons to follow, and Fargo stayed back and watched. Two of Bansen's men were in the other wagons, including the chuck wagon as they passed.

"Go straight into the canyon," Fargo called to Burt Davis and then to Bansen. "It narrows a little," he said. "Your boys stay up front. I'll bring up the rear and keep them moving." Bansen nodded and moved forward as Fargo hung back, Ivy at his side. He gave her a long glance and saw thoughts racing behind her eyes, comprehension gathering in her face. Her whispered words were a confirmation.

"Help comes with horns," she said.

"Go to the head of the class," he muttered, and she stayed at his side as he swung in at the rear of the herd. His eyes peered forward, saw that all four wagons were now in front of the herd, and grunted in satisfaction. Bansen's men were riding forward, also, but at the sides of the cattle. Fargo counted off minutes as he peered over the mass of bodies, a veritable wall of restless, bellowing, pushing forms. But he allowed a grim smile to curl inside him as the words echoed in his mind. Help doesn't have one face. It can come in all shapes and forms. This time it was made of sharp, shiny, long horns on three hundred tons of mean, short-tempered beef.

He rode with his eyes locked in a steady gaze forward just beyond the line of wagons. When he saw the end of the canyon come into sight, his hands tightened on the reins. The trees still obscured the wall of rock behind them, but it would be only another minute before those in the wagons realized they were in a box canyon. He leaned to Ivy. "Get to the trees on the side and stay there. When the rocks stop the stampede, they'll turn and charge back this way," he said, then waited another ten seconds as Ivy yanked her horse around and streaked for the oak lining the side of the canyon. Pulling the Colt from his holster, he saw the instant reaction to the first shots he fired, the longhorns stiffening, horns pulling upwards as the shots split the air.

At his next shots, they let out a collective bellow and the slow-moving mass of bodies was suddenly transformed into a charging, roaring explosion of longhorned power. He kept firing, saw Bansen's men nearest him go down as the longhorns stampeded sideways as well as forward, panic and fury propelling them in a charging mass. He could see the wagons at the end of the canyon going over, hear frantic shouts and screams that somehow managed to rise above the bellowing din and thundering hooves of the longhorns. Burt Davis's wagon rose into the air, lifted by a rush of massive heads, caught and impaled by countless horns. As Fargo watched, it upended, came down in a strange, slow-motion turn, splintering before it disappeared from sight.

The charging mass of cattle began to crush onto each other at the end of the canyon, and Fargo saw them start to turn. In what seemed only seconds, they were charging back through the canyon toward him. Pulling the Ovaro around, he started for the oaks at the side where Ivy had gone. A quick glance sent fear shooting through him. The longhorns were coming at him full charge, moving much more quickly than he'd expected they would. The Ovaro, aware of thundering death suddenly only seconds away, summoned an extra burst of power as it raced for the trees. It reached the oaks just as the first line of steers charged past. Inside the oaks, Fargo felt the ground tremble and saw the trees shake as the herd thundered past, their bodies snapping off branches, horns gouging strips of bark. He backed the pinto against the rocks behind the thin line of oak and watched the stampeding herd rush past until the last of them went by.

He waited and listened to the thunderous sound of them as they continued to stampede out of the canyon. They'd slow eventually, scatter into small knots on the flatland outside the canyon, and he drew a deep breath. "Ivy," he called.

"Here," she said, and he moved forward to see her threading her way through the trees. "I was afraid you weren't going to make it," she said, reaching him. "I'm still shaking."

"They turned more quickly than I thought they could," he said. She leaned from the saddle, her hand pressing into his arm.

"I've got to see if it's finished," he said as he reloaded the Colt. "You want to wait here?"

"No, I'll come with you," she said. He nosed the pinto out of the trees, moved slowly down the canyon, and shot a glance at Ivy as they reached three of Bansen's men. Her lips pulled back, and she turned away from the forms that were crushed into almost shapelessness. He reached the chuck wagon. It was a broken, splintered mass of wood and ripped canvas with part of an arm visible from under a wheel that remained intact. The next wagon was even more torn apart, hardly recognizable as a wagon. The end of the canyon rising up in front of him, Fargo swung from the saddle and walked toward what remained of the Davis wagon. He saw Ivy dismount but stay back near the trees as he reached the wagon. Ben Brewster and

Burt Davis lay trampled alongside pieces of the wagon, recognizable only by their blood-soaked clothes.

He stared down at the two lifeless forms, realized he wanted to summon some pity, then realized he couldn't. They would have killed Ivy and himself without a second thought, had ordered others killed. Justice had come at the end of pounding hooves and longhorns. It was over, he murmured. But he was wrong. Ivy's short half scream told him so, and he spun, saw her on her knees, Lila standing behind her, holding the big Joslyn at her head. "Drop the gun," Lila said. "Now, or she's dead." Fargo stared at Lila Davis. Her face was streaked with dirt, forehead bruised, her blouse all but ripped from her, deep breasts swaying as she took hard breaths. In her eyes he saw the wildness that could snap at any instant. Slowly, he lifted the Colt from its holster and dropped it on the ground. "Kick it away," she ordered, and he obeyed, sending the gun skittering into the splintered debris of the wagon.

"Glad to see you alive, Lila," Fargo said soothingly.

"Shit you are," Lila rasped. "I was thrown into the trees and stayed there."

"I am glad for you, really," Fargo insisted, placatingly.

Lila snarled, and Ivy cried out as she was yanked to her feet by her hair. "Get his lariat," Lila ordered. Ivy's eyes went to Fargo, terror and uncertainty in their depths.

"Do as the lady says," he told her, and she walked to the Ovaro and brought back the lariat. Gesturing with the heavy revolver, Lila motioned to the nearest tree as she hissed words at Fargo.

"Lie there, under that low branch," she ordered. "Do it or I blow your head off now."

"And if I do?" Fargo asked.

"You get to live. You even get to enjoy yourself," Lila said, and he frowned at her, but she didn't say more. He shrugged, strode to the tree, and lay under the branch. He had to buy time. There was rage, pain, and a frightening intensity in Lila's eyes. He had to obey for now, try to find a moment. "Put your arms over your head," she commanded, and he raised his arms. She kept the revolver trained on him as she barked at Ivy. "Tie his arms to the branch with the lariat," she said. Again, Ivy hesitated, unwilling to obey, yet in terror. "Do it or I kill him now," Lila snarled.

"You heard the lady," Fargo said, and Ivy stepped to him, began to tie his wrists together, then bind him to the branch, his arms stretched over his head.

"Tight," Lila bit out, stepped closer, and peered at the knot Ivy had tied. "That'll do. Get back over there," she said, and Ivy moved away. Lila stepped to Fargo, and peered down at him. Still holding the big Joslyn, she pulled his belt open and yanked his Levi's and drawers from him. Her lips drew back in a grimace of a smile. "You know what's going to happen now, you bastard?" she hissed. "I'm going to get my way. I'm going to get what I always wanted." She came closer, stood over him, her eyes burning with an insane light. "You're going to fuck me, just as I said you would."

"You're crazy," Fargo said.

"No, I'm just going to get what I want. I always get what I want. I told you that the first time we met."

He stared up at her. She had always been obsessed, but now there was something more. Now she was insane. She had crossed from obsessed to insane. Maybe it hadn't taken much for her to cross that line, but she had crossed it. She whirled to where Ivy looked on. "And you're going to watch," Lila said. "You're going to watch." She laughed, a wild triumphal laugh as she looked down at Fargo, and then suddenly she whirled at Ivy again. "No, you might enjoy watching," she said. Fargo saw her finger begin to tighten on the trigger of the pistol, and he shouted. Ivy flung herself sideways in a twisting dive, but Lila fired, the heavy sound reverberating in the canyon. He groaned as he saw Ivy's figure tumble as the bullet struck.

"Goddamn you," he cursed at Lila, and she turned back to him. "You still lose. I'm no machine. I can't do it like this."

Lila's eyes glittered. "You'll do it. I'll see to that," she said. She stepped closer, tore off what was left of her clothes to stand over him, legs outspread, deep breasts swaying, her hair in disarray, her full, voluptuous, naked body glistening with perspiration. Suddenly, she was a satanic angel, a Dionysiac goddess, a succubus, Circe, all the myths and legends of famed wantonness come alive. With disdain, she flung the pistol to the ground behind her and dropped to one knee. He pulled on the branch over his head, but the knot at his wrists stayed tight. Lila's eyes blazed with the desire of obsession triumphant, and he felt her hand close around him.

She began to rub, caress, move her hand with long, slow strokes, circle and tickle, stroke again and again. "Yes, yes . . . ah . . . ah . . . aaaah," she breathed, cooed in rhythm with her stroking caresses. He cursed with disbelief as he realized his flesh was beginning to respond, the senses reacting, the body obeying its own impulses, rejecting everything but itself, demonstrating the power of the flesh over the mind. "Ah . . . aaaah . . . aaah," Lila whispered as she stroked, fingers working, exciting, and then her lips, encompassing, vanquishing the last, infinitesimal resistance to the flesh. He heard her sudden triumphal scream as she brought herself down on him. "Yes, yes, now, now, you bastard, now," she cried out, half laughing, half gasping. He tried to twist from under her, but she had him pinned. She was beginning to pump her pelvis up and down when another voice shattered the moment.

"No, get off him, you crazy bitch," Ivy's voice shouted. Fargo turned his head, saw her on one knee, the side of her shoulder stained with red. She held the Joslyn with both hands, pointed at Lila. Lila fell from him, spun, and her scream was a cry of overwhelming rage. Using her strong legs, she flung her full body at Ivy, mad fury propelling her. Her body cut off his view, but he heard the revolver go off, once, then another shot. Lila's fleshy form jiggled, dropped forward, and rolled away. Fargo saw the two big holes pouring scarlet from her midsection. She shuddered and lay still.

He looked at Ivy, saw the horror in her face as she let the revolver drop from her hands. "You had to do it," he said crisply as he saw shock forming in her eyes. "You had to do it, do you hear me?" he repeated. Ivy brought her eyes to him. "Untie me," he said, and she rose, went to the ropes, and in seconds he felt the knot loosen. He drew his clothes up, pushed to his feet, and brought her into his arms. "It was the only way," he said as she clung to him. "She was mad.

153

She'd snapped. It was the only way. She'd have killed me when she finished. I know it."

Ivy lifted her face to his. "Take me away from here," she murmured, and he led her to her horse, climbed onto the Ovaro, and slowly rode from the canyon. He looked at her shoulder as they halted at the other end of the canyon. "The shot grazed me, but it knocked me sideways. It took me a few minutes to pull myself together. When I did, I saw her with you. She was too busy to pay attention to anything else. I crawled on my stomach till I reached the gun."

"You had to do it," he repeated. "You saved my neck."

"You saved us with the stampede," Ivy said. "Let's ride, as far away from here as we can get."

"Good idea," he said and rode southeast with her until the night pushed aside the day and he found a small pond with a big black willow. She undressed, slept with her body tightly pressed against him, as if she could make them become one. In the morning she came from the pond, beautifully naked, droplets of water on the tips of each hardly raised pink nipple.

"I want," she murmured. "But I need another day. I'm still sort of shaken."

"You don't need excuses," he said. "Besides, I want you to come with me. There's a visit I want to make." She dressed and rode with him in silence, and he saw the tiny furrow that stayed on her brow as she wrestled with her own thoughts. He made no effort to intrude, and it was late afternoon when he drew up at Abby Hall's place. Two of the men he recognized were there, working on the barn.

Abby's wan face was apprehensive as she probed

his eyes. "You come to arrest us?" she asked, her glance going to Ivy.

"Is that what you expect?" Fargo returned.

Her shoulders lifted in resignation. "We figured it might happen," she said.

"You did wrong and there was wrong done to you," Fargo said. "I figure there's been more than enough punishment to go around. What's done is done, and I'm not for turning back clocks. There's going to be a new land office agent come here one of these days, and he'll be telling you about a law that lets you buy your land in advance of any auctions if you've worked it. You're getting the chance for a fresh start."

Abby's eyes widened, and he saw the two men looking on with hope flooding their faces. "We'll do right," Abby said.

"Tell all the others," Fargo said.

"We will," one of the men said.

"If you ride north, you'll find a lot of stray long-horns for the taking if you've a mind," Fargo said.

Abby's eyes met his. "I'm sorry about almost everything," she said. He nodded, then let his eyes smile back before he rode away with Ivy. They were moving down a forest pathway as dusk descended, and he found an arbor in which to bed down on a carpet of star moss.

"What did she mean she was sorry about *almost* everything?" Ivy asked.

"We were sort of friends once. Guess she wanted me to know she wasn't sorry about that," Fargo answered casually. He saw Ivy turn the answer in her mind for a moment and decide to accept it. "You were thinking pretty hard when we were riding this morning. Want to talk about it?" he asked.

She gave a rueful little smile. "Guess I was trying to understand myself," she said. "When I got the pistol, I could have thought a lot of things. I could have thought that Lila had to be stopped, that she had tried to kill me and would try again, that she was a madwoman who would kill you."

"You'd have been right with any of those."

"But that's it. I didn't think any of those things. All I thought was that she had some nerve trying to make love to you, trying to take my place. I think I might have shot her even if she hadn't come at me," Ivy said.

"You'll always wonder about that," Fargo said and watched her slip her shirt off.

"Doing is much better than wondering," she said. He agreed as his mouth found hers and his hand curled around her warm roundness.

LOOKING FORWARD!
The following is the opening section from the next novel in the exciting *Trailsman* series from Signet:

THE TRAILSMAN #186
BLUE SIERRA RENEGADES

*1860, the village of Corazon, Old Mexico—
where the parched mountains are blue as cool water,
where bitterness and greed simmer
in the heart of every man and every woman.*

It isn't every day a man gets to go to his own funeral.

On that July afternoon, just after the time for *siesta*, the sun was heading down toward the rim of the barren and almost impassable mountains that surrounded the high desert plain. Slanting light, filtered by dust in the thin air, washed the color of unpolished brass across the rutted road between the adobes that made up the sleepy village of Corazon.

A tall stranger rode slowly into town on a clopping gray. The horse's hooves kicked up small fans of dust. Something about the man made the people of Corazon pause and look. Maybe it was the power of his broad shoulders beneath the tattered wool serape. Or the way his hands held the reins with such assurance. Or the angle of his dark, battered hat, pulled low to hide most of his face so that all that could be seen was a dark, bearded chin.

Or maybe they stopped to stare at the black-and-white pinto, with the rare pattern that marked it as an Ovaro. He was leading it behind him. It was a magnificent horse with a deep chest, powerful legs, and splendid head, the kind of horse that once glimpsed, was not easily forgotten. Across the pinto's back lay a dead man tied to the saddle, facedown, his legs and arms dangling. Dead men were a common sight in Corazon. This one was a gringo in Levi's and a leather vest. Blood dripped from his head, leaving a dotted trail down the street. A Colt glittered in the dead man's holster. A lot of good it would do him now.

The tall stranger in the serape brought both horses to a halt and dismounted. He stood before the cantina, a large adobe building with a wooden portico surmounted by a thatch of ocatillo branches. He shouted out something, a gringo greeting of some kind. By now, everyone in town had gathered around. The old men in sombreros who had been gossiping by the well came hurrying over. Women holding baskets on their hips, put them down and gathered in a knot of colorful cotton skirts, whispering to one another. Some young boys approached shyly, craning their necks to see the dead man's face. One boy dashed up close, reached out a tentative hand to touch the shoulder of the dead man. The dangling arm swung back and forth, and the boy skittered away in alarm.

The tall stranger narrowed his blue eyes and looked around. He seemed to be waiting for something. Several sheepherders emerged from the cantina with glasses of tequila in hand and gazed curiously at the new arrival. They were followed by a woman, tall with long flowing hair that glittered like black fire. Two sharply intelligent eyes flashed beneath dramatically thick brows. A tangle of colorful beads fell across her chest, past the plunging neckline of her cotton blouse, into the deep valley of her cleavage. She wore a shawl embroidered all over with flaming orange, yellow, and scarlet flowers. The fringe swept around her as she lifted her hand to shade her eyes.

"*Buenas días*," the stranger said, addressing her. He spoke Spanish slowly but intelligently with a gringo accent. "This is the village of Corazon?"

She looked around at the sheepherders with a grin, then nodded at the gringo.

"Who's in charge here?"

"I am Rita. This is *my* cantina," the woman answered. She winked at the men standing behind her. They raised their glasses and laughed.

"*Sí, sí!* Rita's in charge here," one of them called out.

"How about a sheriff?" the tall man said, ignoring them. "Got any judge or lawman here in Corazon?"

That brought another round of laughter from the men standing in front of the cantina. Rita raised her eyebrows disdainfully. She stood with one hand on her hip.

"Sheriff?" she repeated. "In Corazon? Ha!"

The tall man crossed impatiently to one of the wooden portico posts where someone had nailed a fresh handbill. The paper fluttered in the slight breeze. He ripped it off and waved it overhead.

"What about this?" he asked them all. "It says here there's a bounty on this man's head. It says to deliver the corpse to Corazon." He pointed to the dead man draped across the back of the Ovaro. "I killed him. And now I'm entitled to that reward. Now if you don't have a sheriff, who's going to pay me?"

A short stocky man stepped out of the group in front of the cantina. He wore rough clothes, all home-spun, all black. A rope belt held his trousers, but his gaze was steady and proud. The late afternoon sun gleamed on his balding head as he descended the steps and drew close to the waiting pinto. Grabbing the back of the hair of the dead man, the sheepherder pulled the hanging head upward.

The villagers gasped. The visage was a dark bloody mass. No nose, no eyes, no mouth. He'd been shot in the face. More than once. The stocky man touched the silver Colt in the dead man's holster, then stroked the flank of the pinto. It shifted away from his touch.

"*Sí, sí.* This is him," the stocky man announced. "I've never seen him, but I've heard the stories. This is his gun and his horse. This is him. This is Skye Fargo. That man they called the Trailsman."

The townspeople muttered to themselves, staring with renewed interest at the body. So this dead man was the famous Trailsman, Skye Fargo, the gringo wanderer who fought a thousand fights, loved a thousand women, found the trails that others could only dream about. And now he was dead.

"That's right," the tall stranger said. "And I had a

devil of a time tracking him down." He held up the piece of paper again. "It says here there's sixty silver doubloons for the man who kills Skye Fargo and brings his body into Corazon. Well, I've done it. So, you'd better tell me right now. Where's my reward? Who's going to pay me?"

"What's your name, stranger? You *Americano*?" Rita asked. She played with the fringe on her shawl.

"Sure, *Americano*," the tall man snapped. His eyes were as cold blue as lake water. He pulled off his battered hat and raked his fingers through his dark hair. "My name's Lawton. Rob Lawton." He seemed to be running out of patience. "Now, here's the corpse of the Trailsman. Where's my goddamn money?"

"*Señor* Lawton, there is no need to be angry," Rita said hastily. "The man who will pay you is named Diego Segundo. He lives . . ." she waved her hands toward the Blue Sierras. "He lives up there, in the mountains. Often he comes to my cantina. I'm sure now you are here, he will come soon. News travels very fast here. Diego will hear you have killed this Trailsman. And he will come to pay you."

"All right then," the gringo answered. "That's better. I just want to be sure I'm going to get my money."

"*Sí, sí,*" Rita said. "You will get your money. While you are waiting, come inside and have a drink. Diego Segundo will be here soon. I am sure."

The man who called himself Rob Lawton tipped his hat to Rita, then followed her inside. A few minutes later, after getting a look at the dead Trailsman, the townspeople dispersed. The men went back inside for another tequila. The women hoisted their baskets on their hips and disappeared. The old men wandered off to their homes.

Only the pack of small boys remained behind. They gathered around the tall pinto. They had heard many many stories about this gringo. Sometimes they had played games pretending to be the mysterious man who was said to be so good he could track a shadow. Now he was dead. And in Corazon. They stood in a silent circle and watched as the blood slowly dripped into the dusty street from the corpse of Skye Fargo, the famous Trailsman.

The cantina was a large whitewashed room filled with rude tables and chairs. Wool blankets striped in green, blue, and orange decorated the walls. *Ristras*, braids of dried red chiles, hung in rows over the bar, which was lined with dusty bottles of clear tequila.

The tall stranger had taken a chair in the corner where he sat by himself. His mouth felt full of trail dust, but a couple of tequilas took care of that. Then he ordered some food. Rita brought him a large platter of enchiladas and stuffed peppers. He smiled up at her, appreciating her flashing dark eyes and brows, her tall full-breasted figure, and narrow waist. It'd been a long ride, he thought.

"Join me for a drink?"

"*Gracias, Señor* Lawton," she had said, "But I am busy." Her eyes traveled across his broad shoulders, lingered on his mouth, searched out the blue eyes beneath the brim of his hat. "Maybe later." It was said with a smile. "I must take care of my customers."

"Call me Rob," he'd answered with a grin as she

whirled away through the crowded room, a glance over her shoulder.

All the time he drank and ate, his eyes silently took in everything about the cantina, about those who came and went. He already knew Corazon was a poor isolated village, high in the Blue Sierras, deep in the *Sierra Madres*. To get to the village, he'd had to travel through the treacherous *Sangre* pass, the only route in and out of Corazon. All around the little village, the land was poor, the dusty hills mottled with black greasewood, ocatilla, cholla cactus, and squawbush. There wasn't much water, just one spring that came out of the mountains and trickled across the brown landscape. Only sheep did well in parched country like this.

The men in the cantina were all herders, dressed in black with weather-roughened faces and woven wool serapes thrown about their shoulders. Occasionally, they glanced over at him curiously, but no one disturbed his solitude. After a couple of hours, he knew he'd got a feel for the village of Corazon. But there were some things he wanted to know that he couldn't find out just by watching. Like why Diego Segundo had wanted him, yeah, Skye Fargo, dead. How long would he have to wait before Segundo arrived, he wondered.

By midnight, the sheepherders were slowly trickling out the door. The stocky herder who'd pronounced the dead man as the Trailsman was passing by his table.

"Buy you a drink?" It was worth a try. Maybe he

could get some information out of him. The sheep-herder pulled up short and looked him over once.

"*Sí, sí, gracias, señor—*"

"Lawton," he gave the name again and reached out his hand, American style. "My name's Rob Lawton. I've come down from Fort Worth, Texas."

"Ramirez," the herder said, awkwardly shaking and pulling up a chair. "Alonzo Ramirez."

He smiled at Alonzo and signaled to Rita to bring tequila and another glass. As she set the bottle in front of him, he noticed her examining him again with interest, flirtatious. She disappeared back into the kitchen.

"Beautiful woman," he remarked.

"She's my sister," Alonzo answered, as if warning him off. The herder was staring hard at him now, as if trying to read him. "Many men have tried to kill Skye Fargo," Alonzo Ramirez said at last, "but you are the one who has succeeded. Never did I think our little town of Corazon would be the place where this famous man came to the end of his trail."

"Yeah." He took a swig of tequila, letting it slowly trickle down his throat. "I always heard Fargo was supposed to be a good fellow. Of course, business is business. And I gotta make money just like the next guy. But I was wondering how come there was a bounty on Fargo's head? Those notices I saw posted all around Chihuahua didn't say anything about why he ought to be killed."

"This Trailsman was a man for hire," Alonzo said, shrugging as if that explained everything.

"So?"

"You paid him some money, he found you a trail.

Or he tracked down somebody who did not want to be found. Nobody in the town of Corazon wanted Skye Fargo to come here."

"Nobody?"

Alonzo took another swig of the liquor and his face was dark, brooding.

"Somebody in Corazon or around Corazon must have hired him," he persisted, trying to get more information out of the herder. "Otherwise, what was he doing way down here in Mexico?" Alonzo remained silent. From the look on his face, he knew something, but he wasn't talking. "What about this guy who's going to pay me for killing Skye Fargo? The one who put up all those notices? Tell me about Diego Segundo—"

At the name, Alonzo stood suddenly. His eyes flickered like lightning in a dark thundercloud. "This man, I do not even speak his name," Alonzo spat. The sheepherder whirled about and left the cantina hurriedly without another word.

Rita reappeared at the kitchen door and, seeing Alonzo's empty place and his abandoned glass of tequila, hurried over, a question in her face.

"I think I offended your brother, Alonzo," he explained to her. "I asked him about Diego Segundo."

"Diego and Alonzo," she said thoughtfully, her eyes on the doorway where her brother had disappeared. "They never liked each other. All their lives."

Maybe he could get some information out of her. A woman like Rita Ramirez who ran the town's only cantina would hear a lot of local gossip. She'd know everything that happened in the valley and in the village of Corazon.

"You must have time for a drink now," he said, glancing around the mostly empty cantina, his eyes coming to rest on the jumble of brilliant beads that hung between her breasts. She smiled at his frankness, lowered herself slowly into the chair, and played with the fringe on her shawl as her dark gaze traveled over him.

"*Señor* Lawton. I have never heard this name before."

"No reason you should. I been keeping myself up in Texas mostly."

"But a man like you, so powerful, so talented with the gun. You must be very very good to kill Skye Fargo," Rita Ramirez said. "Very very good."

"Actually, I'm very bad." He flashed her a grin.

"I don't think you're so bad, *Señor* Lawton. There is something in your face I like very much." Rita bit her lip and leaned over the table with a rattle of beads. Her breasts were tawny mounds beneath the white cotton of her blouse. "Just how bad are you?"

He took a swig of the tequila, then took her chin in his hand, kissed her suddenly, parted her lips with his tongue, let the hot liquor flow from his mouth into hers. She sputtered in surprise, then drank it in, responding to his searching tongue. Then she pulled away with a laugh and shook her hooped earrings. He poured her a drink.

"I see. You are very bad." She laughed.

"Maybe *you* can tell me something about this Segundo fellow," he said, handing her the glass.

"Maybe," Rita said. Her dark eyes held promises of more than just talk.

From outside the cantina came a clamor of men's voices, a jingle of bridles, the creak of leather saddles, then the heavy tread of boots. Suddenly, the figure of a man was towering in the doorway, his eyes sweeping the room. He was close to six feet tall with ringlets of ebony hair, a chiseled face with a slash of angry mouth. His eyes were hard as obsidian. He wore black like the sheepherders, but around his hips were strapped several holsters with carved silver *vaquero* pistols. A bandelero filled with bullets crossed his chest. Damned impressive.

"That's Diego," Rita said to him under her breath. Diego's eyes found his and in answer, he rose slowly to his feet, touched his fingertips lightly to the butt of his pistol. "You can ask him yourself," she added as she fled to the kitchen.

Diego Segundo's men crowded into the cantina after him. They were armed to the teeth, he noticed, but their pistols were of a kind that had been made about a decade before. Not as dependable as the new American-made models, but just as deadly at close range anyway. The few herders who remained in the cantina silently rose and slipped out the door.

"You must be *Señor* Lawton," Diego Segundo said after a long silence. He didn't speak loudly, yet his voice carried clearly. "You are the one who killed Skye Fargo?"

"I sure am." He kept his voice hard-edged, his fingers on the pistol butt, every nerve in his body alert, ready. "And I'm looking for that reward. You the one who's going to pay me?"

Diego Segundo made his way toward him, their eyes locked. When they were face-to-face, Diego Segundo smiled very slowly, then suddenly reached over and clapped him on the shoulder.

"*Bueno, bueno*," Diego said, his eyes glittering. "*Señor* Lawton, first I buy you a drink. We will be friends. I want to talk to the man who killed the famous Trailsman."

Diego's men all relaxed and began talking, taking seats all around the room. Rita brought drinks and food. Diego Segundo sat across the table with a big smile on his face, seemingly relaxed, expectantly waiting to hear the story of how Skye Fargo was killed. But behind his eyes, Diego Segundo seemed watchful as a starving cougar. Diego's piercing gaze would miss nothing. This story would have to be good. Good and convincing.

"I hadn't planned on being down in Mexico," he got around to saying after they exchanged a few preliminaries. "Only I got in some trouble up in Fort Worth." He kept his voice low, as if he didn't want anybody else to hear. "Shot up the sheriff's brother good. So I thought I'd come south for a while. Got as far as Chihuahua and ran out of cash." He paused and took a swallow, felt its long burn down his gullet. Diego was hanging on his every word. "Saw your notices up and thought I could sure use sixty silvers. Somebody said they'd seen a fellow that looked like Fargo riding south out of Chihuahua on a black-and-white pinto. So I followed him. Was heading up into the Blue Sierras, right toward this village."

"How did you shoot him?" Diego asked.

"Got lucky, really. We'd had a long ride all day, and I was following him about a mile behind. He'd never even spotted me. I waited until the middle of the night and just sneaked up on his camp. Campfire was still going, so I had enough light to see him sleeping there. I've got a good rifle, and I'm a pretty good aim, so I didn't have to get real close. Knew I had one shot. If I missed, it was good-bye sixty silvers. But I got him. Put a window in his skull, and he never woke up. Then I blew him a few more times to make sure. He's dead all right."

"*Bueno, bueno!*" Diego Segundo nodded and smiled, then clapped him on the shoulder again. Yeah, Diego had bought the story. Didn't seem suspicious in the least. Diego rose and motioned for him to follow. His rest of the men crowded out after them. Outside the cantina, darkness blanketed the town, but there was enough silvery light from the half moon to see by. The Ovaro still stood with the dead man hanging across its back.

"Pull him off," Diego instructed his men. They did so, and in a moment the corpse lay in the dusty street, the bloody mess that had once been a face turned toward the stars.

Diego called to one of his men who brought a buckskin bag that clinked with coins. Diego handed it over. He opened it, counted the money, then drew the pouch shut and pocketed it.

"Well, that makes us even. But I've got one question. Why'd you want him dead?"

"Skye Fargo was a troublemaker," Diego answered, patting the Ovaro's withers appreciatively. The horse shifted uneasily. Just as Diego bent down and started to retrieve the Colt out of the dead man's holster, he stuck out his foot and planted his boot on the dead man's gun before Diego could grasp it. The others standing around gasped and took a threatening step forward.

"The notice said to deliver Skye Fargo dead for sixty silvers," he said to Diego. He put the hard edge in his voice again. "The way I figure it, the gun and the horse and all Fargo's gear belong to me now." Diego straightened and stared him down for a long moment. "You paid for the corpse. I get the rest."

"You're one tough gringo," Diego said. "A horse like this is very valuable. The guns, too." Diego touched the Henry rifle in the saddle scabbard longingly. There was something else in his voice now. Respect. Curiosity. An undertone of suspicion. "You're a very valuable man, *Señor* Lawton. Obviously a sure shot, too. Maybe you'd like to ride with us for a while. Make some more silver. You could use money?"

"I sure could."

"And I could use another good gun right now," Diego said.

Yeah, Diego was suspicious now. Wanted to keep an eye on him. But this was better than he'd bargained for. A chance to ride with Diego and his gang, find out about the gang. But first he needed to get a message to the rancher, Cassidy Donohue.

"Sure," he said. "But I need a day's rest first. It's been a long ride."

"Of course," Diego said smoothly. "Tomorrow we meet you up there—" he pointed to the dark shapes of the Blue Sierras against the night sky. "Tomorrow morning, you ride to the foothills. We will find you. *Buenos noches.*"

In another moment Diego and his men mounted and rode out like shadows in the night. The dead man lay still in the middle of the street. Corazon was quiet under the half-moon.

He untethered the Ovaro and the big gray and led the horses toward the watering trough for a drink. Then he walked back into the cantina, only to find it deserted. Rita was gone. He swore to himself. Corazon was too small a village to have a hotel. He propped a chair against the wall in front of the cantina and caught a few hours' sleep.

At dawn, the blazing sun ascended fast, a white disc on the bleached sky. It was going to be a scorcher. He stretched his arms overhead. Time to get a move on.

An old man with a shovel over his shoulder was walking up the street and paused to look at the dead man. He rose out of the chair in front of the cantina, thinking it was as good a time as any to get the body buried. The old man spotted him then, started in surprise as he pulled one of the silver coins from the leather pouch, and offered it. Together they lifted the dead man back onto the pinto and led it, along with the gray, down the short dusty street and out beyond the little adobes. The ground was too hard to dig a grave, so they piled a rock cairn over the dead body.

When they'd finished, the old man removed his hat and seemed to be saying a prayer. He crossed himself, then walked away with the shovel over his shoulder, toward the village. The sun was higher now, and Corazon was starting to stir.

The tall man with the lake-blue eyes mounted the Ovaro and sat looking down for a moment at the rock cairn. It wasn't every day a man gets to go to his own funeral.

He had no idea who the dead man had been. Some unlucky bastard, a drifter trying to make a quick buck. All he knew was that the stranger had tried to ambush him. And in his pocket had been the handbill offering a reward for the death of Skye Fargo.

As Skye Fargo rode away from Corazon on the black-and-white pinto, he knew his life now depended on Diego Segundo continuing to believe that the Trailsman was dead and gone. His name was Rob Lawton now, he told himself. Rob Lawton from Fort Worth, Texas.

He crossed the stream, a trickle of water over brown stones, bordered by cottonwood trees not far from town. He'd gone three more miles and was cantering northward toward a long line of dry hills when he turned about in the saddle to check on the gray. It was keeping up nicely. His keen eyes swept the land behind him. Against the illumination of the low slant of morning sun, he spotted the subtle telltale smudge of dust rising a mile or so back.

Yeah, Diego Segundo was suspicious of the Texan named Rob Lawton all right. So suspicious, he was having him followed.

Ⓢ SIGNET

LEGENDS OF THE WEST

☐ **SCARLET PLUME by Frederick Manfred.** Amid the bloody 1862 Sioux uprising, a passion that crosses all boundaries is ignited. Judith Raveling is a white woman captured by the Sioux Indians. Scarlet Plume, nephew of the chief who has taken Judith for a wife, is determined to save her. But surrounded by unrelenting brutal fighting and vile atrocities, can they find a haven for a love neither Indian nor white woman would sanction? (184238—$4.50)

☐ **RIDERS OF JUDGMENT by Frederick Manfred.** Full of the authentic sounds and colors of the bloody Johnson County range wars of the 1890s, this tale of Cain Hammett and his devotion to his family and his land, captures the heroism of a long-vanished era. When the cattle barons invade Cain's territory, this man of peace must turn to his guns and avenge all that has been taken from him. "A thriller all the way."—*New York Times* (184254—$4.99)

☐ **WHITE APACHE by Frank Burleson.** Once his name was Nathanial Barrington, one of the finest officers in the United States Army. Now his visions guide him and his new tribe on daring raids against his former countrymen. Amid the smoke of battle and in desire's fiercest blaze, he must choose between the two proud peoples who fight for his loyalty and the two impassioned women who vie for his soul. (187296—$5.99)

☐ **WHISPERS OF THE MOUTAIN by Tom Hron.** White men had come to Denali, the great sacred mountain looming over the Indians' ancestral land in Alaska, searching for gold that legend said lay hidden on its heights. A shaman died at the hands of a greed-mad murderer—his wife fell captive to the same human monster. Now in the deadly depth of winter, a new hunt began on the treacherous slopes of Denali—not for gold but for the most dangerous game of all. (187946—$5.99)

☐ **WHISPERS OF THE RIVER by Tom Hron.** Passion and courage, greed and daring—a stirring saga of the Alaskan gold rush. With this rush of brawling, lusting, striving humanity, walked Eli Bonnet, a legendary lawman who dealt out justice with his gun . . . and Hannah Twigg, a woman who dared death for love and everything for freedom. (187806—$5.99)

*Prices slightly higher in Canada

THE WILD FRONTIER

☐ **JUSTIS COLT by Don Bendell.** The Colt Family Saga continues, with the danger, passion, and adventure of the American West. When Texas Ranger Justis Colt is ambushed by a gang of murderers, a mysterious stranger, Tora, saves his life. But now the motley crew of outlaws demand revenge and kill Tora's wife and two sons. Vengeance becomes a double-edged sword as Colt and Tora face the challenge of hunting down the killers.
(182421—$4.99)

☐ **THE KILLING SEASON by Ralph Compton.** It was the 1870s—and the West was at its wildest. One man rode like a legend of death on this untamed frontier. His name was Nathan Stone, and he has learned to kill on the vengeance trail. He would have stopped after settling the score with his parents' savage slayers. But when you are the greatest gunfighter of all, there is no peace or resting place. . .
(187873—$5.99)

☐ **THE HOMESMAN by Glendon Swarthout.** Briggs was an army deserter and claim jumper who was as low as a man could get. Mary Bee Cuddy was a spinster homesteader who acted like she was as good as any man. Together they had to take back east four women who had gone out of their minds and out of control. "An epic journey across the plains . . . as good as novels get."—
Cleveland Plain Dealer
(190319—$5.99)

*Prices slightly higher in Canada

Buy them at your local bookstore or use this convenient coupon for ordering.

PENGUIN USA
P.O. Box 999 — Dept. #17109
Bergenfield, New Jersey 07621

Please send me the books I have checked above.
I am enclosing $_____ (please add $2.00 to cover postage and handling). Send check or money order (no cash or C.O.D.'s) or charge by Mastercard or VISA (with a $15.00 minimum). Prices and numbers are subject to change without notice.

Card #_____ Exp. Date _____
Signature_____
Name_____
Address_____
City _____ State _____ Zip Code _____

For faster service when ordering by credit card call **1-800-253-6476**

Allow a minimum of 4-6 weeks for delivery. This offer is subject to change without notice.